TOP STORIES

EDITED BY ANNE TURYN

CITY LIGHTS BOOKS

SAN FRANCISCO

©1991, Top Stories

Book and cover design by Rex Ray

Library of Congress Cataloging-in-Publication Data

Top top stories / edited by Anne Turyn
    p.   cm.
    Selections from the prose journal Top stories.
    ISBN 0–87286–258–5 : $9.95
    1. Short stories, American.   2. American fiction—20th century.
    I. Turyn, Anne.   II. Top stories.
    PS848.S5T6   1991
    813'.0108054—dc20   91–10325
                                                                      CIP

City Light Books are available to bookstores through our primary dis-
tributor: Subterranean Company, PO Box 168, 265 South 5th Street,
Monroe, OR 97456. Phone: (503) 847-5274. Toll free orders: (800) 274-
7826. Our books are also available through library jobbers and regional
distributors. For personal orders and catalogs, please write to City
Lights Books, 261 Columbus Avenue, San Francisco, CA 94133. Phone:
(415) 362-8193.

CITY LIGHTS BOOKS are edited by Lawrence Ferlinghetti & Nancy
J. Peters and published at the City Lights Bookstore, 261 Columbus
Avenue, San Francisco, CA 94133.

EDITOR'S NOTE

Why did I start *Top Stories?*
>to provide a forum for non-traditional prose or narrative works
>to create a series
>to feature the work of one author/artist per volume
>to devote a publication to prose
>to allow each author/artist maximum input on the design of their volume
>to make public and affordable certain texts

I would like to thank all the individuals and organizations that helped to make *Top Stories* possible. Thanks to Hallwalls, Hard Press, Arts Development Services Regrant Program (Buffalo), the New York State Council on the Arts (Literature Program), the Coordinating Council of Literary Magazines, the Committee for the Visual Arts (New York City), The Magazine Co-op (New York City), The National Endowment for the Arts, The Beard's Fund, LINE II, and the Department of Cultural Affairs (New York City). Many individuals have contributed time and energy, as well as expertise, to *Top Stories*. I would especially like to thank Laurie Neaman, Gail Vachon and Linda Neaman for all they have done. I am indebted to Nancy Linn, without whose support and devotion there would be no *Top Stories*. Thank you. And thank you to all the *Top Stories* authors/artists.

Anne Turyn
February 1991

Dedicated to the memory of Cookie Mueller

TOP

TOP STORIES

CONTENTS

LINDA NEAMAN

FOOT FACTS

TOP STORIES #5 $2.00

foot
facts

linda
neaman

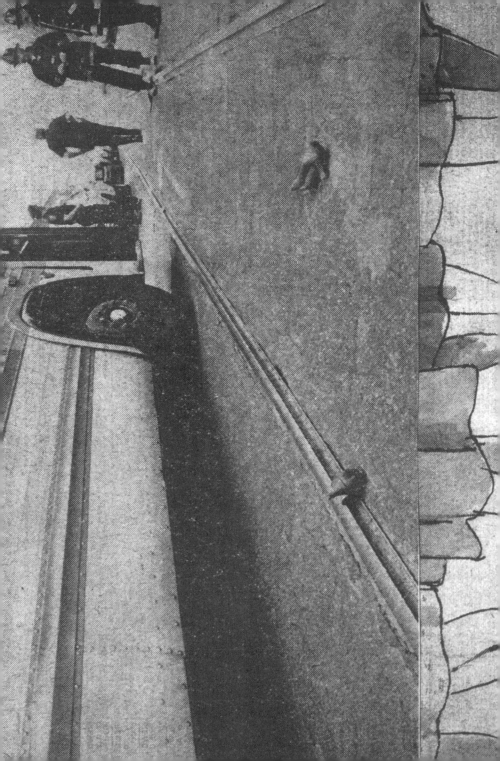

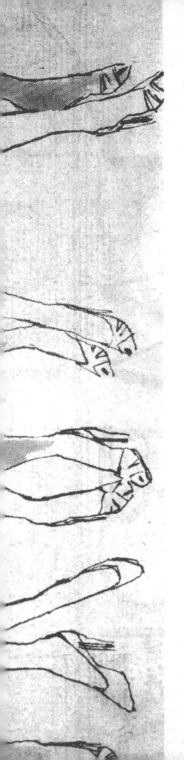

HOW TO WEAR HIGH HEELS

Very high heels tend to jam toes to the front of the shoe. Save them for occasions when you won't be on your feet much. For all-day wear or for evenings of lots of dancing, your best bet is a shoe with a lower heel. When going from a high heel to flat-or from flat to high-do it gradually. Change heel heights during the day, switching from a high heel to a two-incher to a flat, or vice versa. This avoids aching calf muscles. Shop for shoes toward the end of the day when your feet have expanded as much as 5% as a result of heat and activity.

WHAT HIGH HEELS DO TO FEET

Your feet are amazing constructions. Each one contains twenty-six bones linked by thirty-three joints and two hundred ligaments. Your feet walk between seven and a half to ten miles on an average day. In spite of their durability, feet sometimes don't take kindly to high heels. High heels tend to throw most of your weight on the balls of your feet which can cause serious and painful corns and calluses. Wearing high heels for long periods of time can shorten your Achilles tendon and cause it to react painfully when you stretch it by walking barefooted or wearing low heels. Making sure you wear a variety of heel heights will help prevent this.

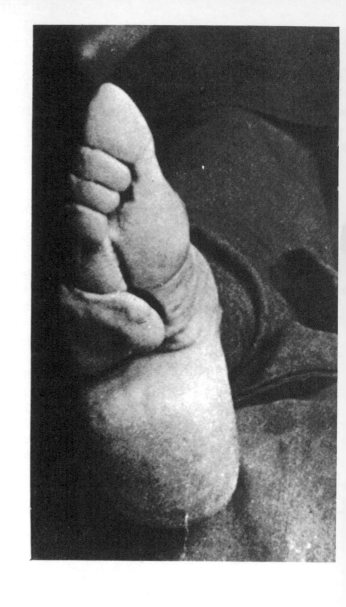

Why must the foot be bound?

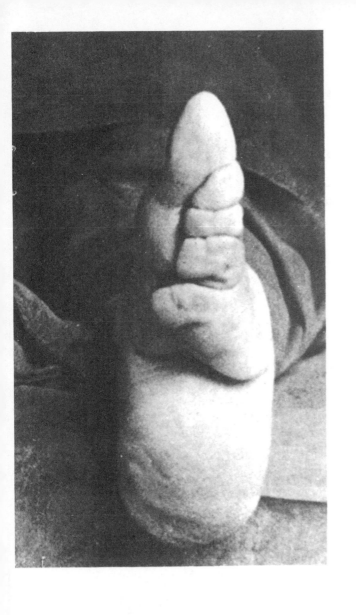

To prevent
barbarous running
around!

REFLEXOLOGY

▲ sinuses   ◆ pituitary

■ neck   ○ throat & tonsils

◉ eyes   ♠ back of head

☾ ear   ✖ stomach

⋈ solar plexus   ⌐ lungs

⬆ shoulder & arm joints

♥ heart   ⬅ pancreas

● spinal vertabrae

◗ kidney   ✓ spleen

✚ bladder   ▼ coccyx

◻ intestines ▮ hip joint

⧖ thigh & knee

ⴸⴸ sciatic nerve

GAIL VACHON

THIS IS MY MOTHER. THIS IS MY FATHER.

THIS IS MY MOTHER.
THIS IS MY FATHER.

This is my mother. This is my father.

I had heard that a new form had been invented.
I went to the grocery store to look for it.
The produce department seemed an appropriate place.
A shortness of breath overcame me.
My brother, who was a medical doctor, was called.
An asparagus or crooked-neck squash was called for and
     produced.
She's not interested.
She's gazing into space.
She thinks what you are saying is boring.
She's repelled by your eagerness.
Her breath returns.
Her produce is gathered into a wire basket; her brother dis-
     missed.
I am also speaking of my ideas, my autobiography, who I know.

My brother is no fool.
He rides the wake and is brought to a conclusion.
He takes the bull by the horns.
His perceptions become razor-sharp.

Alone again, one wanders, the other follows a northerly di-
     rection.
The wanderer takes a deep breath.
The other, my brother, is reminded of his past.
He drinks beer, he reads magazines and sits on his balcony.

* * *

Your wandering leads you to a grassy knoll.
You stretch and gulp.
A deer meets your gaze, and you take out your lunch.
You offer to share your meal; to repeat your gestures.
There is a salty smell, of urine or sweat.
I'm tough, or I'm a pretty girl.
I know what I am saying.

* * *

The northern region is full of wild animals.
At night they make beautiful terrifying sounds.
The streets are narrow and lined with tall ombrous trees.
Many of the houses are painted red; each has a little balcony
     from which, visionless, this night world may be perceived.
A more casual approach can also be taken: magazines can be
     read, refreshments offered, impossible desires forgotten
     and another's anxiety ignored.

Inside the house, my daughter is learning to cook.
Tonight she will make ratatouille.
The dark pup watches from the window.
The vegetables are in several piles.
Music is playing.
My hand brushes against the front of your pants.
The kitchen door is closed tightly.

The airport is a few miles away.
My daughter likes to watch the planes; we go there regularly.
We went to meet an old friend.
She had a new hairstyle.
She was on vacation.
Drinks were ordered for all.
Money slipped through our fingers; I caught my breath; my
    brother consoled me.
Autumn was coming.

* * *

She moved to Germany when we were five.
The father was an opera singer.
The mother was a vegetarian.
They made paper dolls and played doctor.
She got her period before me although she was a year younger.
They wore identical clothing and told people they were sisters.
They dug two deep pits in the woods and filled them with
    blankets.
I don't know why but these were very important, secret sexual
    places.
They dug them together towards the end of their friendship,
    shortly before I went away for the summer.
They had the same birthday, one year apart.

She was two years older than me.
They took drugs together.
We were painters.
They were feminists.
We were lovers.
My extraordinarily intense fear of car crashes seems to be
    diminishing.

I have this brother he's the black sheep of the family.
He's not crazy or anything he's a professional baseball player.
He plays for the Cleveland Indians he got shot in the leg
    because he had so many gambling debts.
I wish I was a waitress.

A story of two lovers.
One falls in love with someone else and shares this with the
    first lover, stating that the older relationship must end.
Together they find a suitable new partner for the first lover
    before ending the relationship.
They discuss the potential new mates' good and bad qualities.

Do you hear the Muzak?
He longs for the threads to be picked up.
Vegetables were strewn about on the floor.
My brother swept things into piles.
She describes attitudes in discreet sentences.
You might go walk in the garden tonight.
They tell me I am clever and lovely.
We are on the way to Montpelior.
She and I dance with cold on the ferry crossing.
We'll be back here again in ten days.
We don't know it but we'll be back.
We'll be here.

I went into the grocery store to get the feeling.
I got crazy with the feeling I danced and whooped with the
    products.
My brother gave me Natural Foods.
I felt so much better.
I was one of the first babies born by Natural Childbirth.
My groceries were all around me.
My brother drank Miller's HiLife.
We're moving to New York.

These African men have a guarded suspicious look in their eyes.
A very fat salesman helps them try on sport coats.
They are an odd size.
The department does not carry odd sizes.

My daughter sat on the balcony.
She was sewing a red dress.
The threads glistened in the fluorescent light.

I am sitting in a rocking chair, reading Look Magazine.
We would go for a swim, but the chlorine gives her a rash.
Or was it the moonlight?
She didn't seem to mind.
I spanked her little bottom.
I've stolen these four minutes, like all others.

Long red scarves are in vogue.
You're my sweetheart.
You have that special something.
You want me to wear high heels and grow my hair long.
You fly in a plane.
Animals nuzzle in your warmth.
You desire certain products.

There has been a robbery at the bakery around the corner.
My brother is driving.
Our breath comes more easily in this northern climate.
He is careful not to run over any animals.
We glide past the darkened grocery store.
Something is making me nervous.
I pluck at a thread on my sleeve.
We listen to music on a Milwaukee radio station.

The baby cries all night.
He cries all night.
The baby, he cries all night.
I'm not getting any sleep.
I fall asleep at odd moments of the day.
We decide to get some help.
I hire a woman to help with the chores.
She doesn't want to take care of the baby.
She eats everything in the refrigerator, and feeds me peanut
    butter.
I don't know what to do.
My friend is sympathetic.
My friend tells me to fire her.
I try to fire her but ask for a glass of water instead.

14

My friend is afraid of her too.
Finally, I get an idea.
I will make a big mess in the house and she will quit.
I spread peanut butter on the kitchen counters.
A man brings old feather pillows and we have a pillow fight.
I hang the pictures crooked.
Everything is ready.
My friend comes in and says, "What's going on here?"
I explain my idea.
My friend, taking pity on me, has just fired the woman.

She walks slowly and I cannot keep up.
She suggests that my tone is too romantic.
Her sentences, on the other hand, are very bitter.
We make a list of possible sources of cynicism: life, smog,
      offices, fashion, television, art, romance, babies.

I visit an old friend.
She tells me, "You look so pretty. Are you very happy? or very sad?"
She doesn't use contractions, or the words "oh," "so," "up."
Her sentences are complete in themselves.

Cakes, cookies, pastries, pies, donuts, tortes fly through the air.
The clerk clutches at her own throat.
She imagines she is remembering this and other good times,
      years hence.
The robber has a black scarf on her face, and a gun.
Crumbs settle on the dollar bills.
The clerk's arms are sticky with chocolate icing.
The robber thinks to linger, but leaves instead with the money.

The sound passes through the throat wasting no breath.
I remember good times, but do I remember only what I have
      always longed for?
Or perhaps I am remembering the future.
As soon as he tells me what the warlock said: that encountering a
      deer is a good omen, I will see deer every time I go into
      the mountains.

We will hear 2 cars smash into each other on the road below.
We will see a boy plummet to his death from a Colorado
　　mountain.
We will not allow things to happen in threes.

She was dark-skinned, about 35.
She wore a black scarf covering the lower half of her face.
The clothes she wore were plain.
She left in a big grey car.

You went uptown for a haircut.
In the mirror you looked hard and misshapen.
The pretty hairdresser asked questions and did not listen to
　　your answers.
She fiddled with the radio.
She danced as she snipped at your hair.

I'm not going to buy nailpolish, or a car or a donut or a
　　typewriter or something to make me blue.
My brother will give me money and something hot to drink.
Your thoughtfulness will pay off.
You'll count your money and ride in an airplane.
People you've never seen will say "How are you?"
Your thoughtfulness will have paid off.

The women executives are very tall.
They carry the money in big suitcases.
I can lend you a few dollars if you're short.
It's a satisfying career.
At lunchtime she sucks on plums and cherries and dreams of a
　　frozen river, elsewhere.

Your mother sat in the corner for ½ an hour with her hand over
　　her eyes.
Your father broke down in the middle.
They give you a 4 week impression five weeks in succession.
They want your money.
They give you things to make you spend your money; gold chain

with signs of the zodiac.
You'll read my mind.

Animals make low groans as he gathers my long hair in his hands.
The Mother of Me says to the Baby of Me, "Do you know what
   you are doing?"
I stare straight ahead.
He pulls my hair back and ties a scarf over my nose and lips.

You work in a bank.
You talk on the telephone.
A co-worker complains of a belly-ache.
Every 15 minutes you get some coffee or urinate.
Your mother's photograph on the desk watches with disap-
   proval.
The air conditioner hums.
They speak French here, in November.
I am dreading November.

If a tree fell in a forest, it would make a deafening roar.
Animals retreat.
A black pup with an artist's name sits listening in front of a plant.
A bloody crowd trips down the steps while the soldiers, carrying
   bayonets, march up.
You'd think I complained all the time.
Can't you hear yourself?

It's a night out with my electric guitar.
My boyfriend yells at me because I messed up the song.
I'm wearing a shiny shirt.
You're wearing shiny shoes.
Some of the songs we sing are in French.
The telephone rings and rings.

She's sitting in an office by a window.
Outside her window is a 30-story building beside a vacant lot.
There is a gap between the north and south halves of the
   building.

17

Little bridges on every floor connect the two halves.
I never see anyone on these little bridges.
The shadows of the buildings on the other side of the lot climb
     down her building; if she were here for a long time she
     would amuse herself by learning to tell time by their
     position.

A lady behind me hums the theme from Looney Tunes.
A man across the way says, "I'm living but I'm not living."
The telephone rings and rings.

She is having a "nervous breakdown."
Two years ago she tried to kill herself.
She slashed her wrists.
I was horrified when I saw her arms.
She hasn't tried to kill herself this year.
My brother says she has too much control of herself.
I guess I have too much consciousness of myself.
It's a long story, too long to go into here.
You promise to take me to the races in the spring.

We take the subway to the racetrack.
We go through the turnstile.
The crowd is milling about.
The horses are led around in a circle.
Several people laugh at the idea of roast beef and swiss cheese.

I admire one of the horses as well as his jockey clad in shiny
pink.
I make a $2 bet on No. 2.
We have pizza and Yoo-hoo.
Her skin looks very dry, as if she lived in New Mexico.
My face is grey and pinched.
After a while you get used to things being this bad.
Like if you have an embarrassing personal problem you don't talk
     to anyone about it and it gets internalized so that you're
hardly
     conscious of it.

Well, theorizing about things is no help at all.
You have to take action.
Hi sweetheart how are you?
I ironed my red shirt and it melted.
I wore it anyway.
I'm driving now.
We enter a tunnel and our pupils contract.
The tunnel is made of shiny white tiles lit by fluorescent lights.
My brother and I sing "One Hundred Bottles of Beer on the
    Wall."

We come out of the tunnel and radio comes back on.
It's dark, we sing about beer, we play the radio.
The tunnel seemed very bright.
The black pup, pink tongue dripping, sits obediently.
The telephone rings and rings.

My daughter visited the arcade.
She bought fish protein concentrate and the clerk smiled
    an archaic smile.
She said she was late because of the arctic wind.
She told this fishy story and smiled archly at my disbelief.
I served her fried fish and french fried potatoes.
I fed the leftovers to the deer.

Is there anymore? Anymore? Is there anymore?
Are you ready? Are you ready for this? Do you like it? Do you
    like it like this?

Fishless waters flow through this arcane place.
Let's take a trip! Let's drive down that old avenue we used to
    know so well.
An old black Buick is still parked by the side of the road.
She lingers there with a queer fish who studies archaeology.
An anathema is a curse.
Your old age is approaching. Are you ready?

I hear there's a very attractive shopping center below street level.

It's so big and there are so many people you don't know.
My horse-racing friend once sold money.
I gave her a miniature doll from Guatemala in exchange for
    20 pennies.

The path snakes its way up the mountain.
Redbirds are all around.
You take off your hat and wipe your brow.
You haven't heard the news in weeks.
You open the window.
It's a long way down; you toss a penny.

Your sweetheart makes you a drink.
You live on the twenty-second floor.
Your windows overlook a huge vacant lot.
There is a fountain across the street.
Red pennies underwater glisten in the sunlight.

Someone met my brother on the bridge and later heard him
    speak his lines with gusto.
They shared an awkward meal.
They attempted to reconcile their 2 languages.
I walked, you rode your bicycle.
They misunderstood each other's sentences.
Sometimes one looked over the other's shoulder when they
    spoke.

I was fingerprinted again this morning.
They made two prints of each finger; one flat and one rolled.
I looked very solemn when they took my picture.
The lady explained that it would be in the FBI's permanent file.

She made a little bow when she walked in front of the store.
I am given a feather.
You are trembling slightly.
We ride to the river and tie our horses at the bridge.
The sky is pink.
You have head lice.

She stretched her long legs and opened a bottle of beer.
She will wear a black scarf with glistening red threads running
    through it.
She disregards the rules and she will pay for it.
I'll turn the heat on for her.

We make an agreement on the telephone.
You acknowledge my influence.
You've lost your receipt and your confidence.

The ladies admire you.
She looks like a little doll.
You look so proud holding her.
But I hear you cursing under your breath.

It's Friday night and the boys are placing their bets.
They're remembering a rare treat.
Red-eyed animals lurk in the bathroom.
You make efficient use of your time.

You sit on the balcony and ponder the future.
An airplane flies overhead.
Confetti flutters down.
You've found your receipt.
You turn the pages languidly.
You're relaxed.
The telephone rings and you do not answer.
Tonight, you can see your breath.

I can hear the water flowing and the soft motions of the horses.
I disregard the rules.
I ride in a short airplane.
Someone will meet me at the airport.
We will have a large meal.
I will be languid and confident.

* * *

I drove my brother's car.
The car ran out of gas.
A handsome guy offered me a ride to the gas station in his van.
When we got there, he pulled out a gun and took the money.

We went screaming down the highway.
We robbed a bakery and a flower shop.
I sang a sexy song in a bar while he robbed the bartender.
When we got outside the police were waiting for us.
My brother was with them.
The guy had a gun but I pulled his hair.
Three policemen ran up and grabbed him.
He said "shit" on television.

I can hear the water flowing and the soft motions of the horses.
I disregard the rules.
I ride in a short airplane.
Someone will meet me at the airport.
We will have a large meal.
I will be languid and confident.

* * *

I haven't mentioned that I make films.
I haven't mentioned that my name is Poland.
I haven't mentioned my children, Jack and Mary.
In New York the workmen play ring-around-the-rosy on
    the girders.
The disco beat catches your step.
The pulse of the nation drives your heart.

He came to the doctor's office for scientific investigation.
The doctor made a speech.
He returned to the hospital two years later wearing a long black
    cape and a bag pulled over his head.
The doctor ran an advertisement in the Sunday paper.
Suitable accommodations were found for him.

He attended the opera; he visited the countryside.
Daily baths eliminated the foul odor.
Beautiful ladies of noble birth touched his hand and gave him
    photographs of themselves.
A short time later, he died in his sleep.

You'll be home tonight you're my sweetheart I've swept the
    floor.
You have that special something.
We'll have a fine meal.
I bought red flowers for the table.

She picks up her threads.
Her senses are in tune.
She puts her gear into the car.
They go ice fishing in New Hampshire.
There's a pile of lemons on the table, a stack of magazines by the
    radio.
Saturday, Wednesday, Friday, Tuesday.

Your tattered fashions will lead you nowhere.
I had heard that a new word had been invented.
You get oh, so dressed up, and go out shopping.
Maybe you would hear it on the street.
My pants zip up the side; I close my jacket zippers.
My high heels grind into the pavement.

What do I want—fame, fortune—what?
You know the answer only when your gears are out of synch.
You wear heels so high you teeter and fall.
It's dangerous and your face is dirty.
You're disorganized and your feet hurt.

You came back together at last, years later.
You compared experiences.
I had become a famous skier, and traveled a lot.
The thin air invigorated me; the alpenglow gave me spiritual
    solace.

You avoided the subject of money.

Her spikey haircut punctured the elevator.
She was disconsolate.
The money she had spent had wiped out her savings.
She sang a funny little song.

In Nova Scotia, I went out to buy a pair of wool trousers.
The store is having an election day special.
The disco beat makes you want to spend your money.
My plans were shattered.
I was disconsolate.
I put my trousers on lay-away.
I bought a Yoo-hoo and sank into a chair.

"Aloha," said a black man selling hot dogs and Yoo-hoo.
I can't help smiling.
I notice the length of skirts, shiny buckles on shoes.
My daughter is throwing her boomerang in the back yard.
She is glad to see me and gulps her chocolate soda eagerly.
I thumb through my magazine, being a mother.

If only I could get a little ahead of myself.
I buy bananas but I only slip and fall.
I plan a ferry crossing.
My brother will pick me up and give me relief.
I'll take the bull by the horns.

A distant cousin from the South has dropped in unexpectedly.
He talks loud and has a funny walk.
His manners are peculiar.
He keeps his money in his shoe.
He goes to bed at 9:15.
He sleeps in the living room, so we have to go to bed too.
He has never been to the city before.
He is wary of bad women, but grateful to us.
We don't know what to do.
He wakes up early and sings country songs.

He is grateful to us for taking care of him.
Finally I get an idea.
I will disguise myself as the woman he fears and he will leave.
I will wear dangly earrings and a low-cut gown.
I will wiggle when I walk.
I enter the room in my costume and approach my cousin.
He is delighted to meet me.
He decides to stay on in the city.

She had asked for directions.
I pointed towards the northwest.
We walked at different paces.
Because I dislike words, I had to walk quickly to keep ahead of
    them.

I'm marking time.
My half-birthday will be in December.
Perhaps you're too old to count your birthdays by halves.
But like my middle name, my half-birthday was revealed to me
    late in life, when I thought I had already been told all the
    facts about myself.
I was 4 and a half at the time.

I love the disco and the natural food.
Disco makes me feel so good.
When I walk down the street the disco comes out of all the stores.
The disco, it's the driving pulse of the nation.
Disco makes you want to buy.

Your old friends are bored with you.
Your new lover hasn't time for you.
Your parents are dead.
Water and gas flow through the pipes.

In front of the bakery across the street from the supermarket,
    you thought you saw a little black and white dog.
You turned, and it was a fire hydrant.
You wonder if you've lost your way.

Your bags are getting heavier.
You can see your breath.
My wife wants to leave the city.
She's going crazy.
She has to get out of New York.
We take the train to the plane.
We take the boat-train.
We take a seaplane.

Exhaust fumes engulf the avenue.
You pull yourself together one last time.
You plan a trip.
You find your way on a map.

Your wife is going crazy.
You breathe.
You stretch and gulp.
Can't you hear yourself?
Your arms are sticky.
Other people have planned their activities carefully.
She smells like a man.

You review the directions.
You make your way through the brush.
Your daughter is at your left side.
The sun is rising behind you to your right.

What kind of a girl do you want to marry, Bob?
Bob was embarrassed.
I'd like a big tall beautiful Irish girl.
She took a big gulp of coke to make herself burp.

She worked in a bank.
Every morning she walked several miles to work.
On holidays they spread the desks with little cakes and
    cookies.
In the mailroom they play disco on the radio.

I'm looking forward to winter sports.
When the snow falls I won't be sorry.
They've decided to announce their engagement.
This seems like a good idea.

They'll serve fruit and cheese.
She wears a gold chain.
We'll remember certain photographs, and try to resemble them.
My elbow hurts.
You know the feeling.

You answer phones and make notes.
You walk from one work station to another.
You verify items.

My wife is going crazy.
I will have to give up my job at the bank.
I have to take her away.

Communication by trance with animals was attempted.
She stared at a swinging pendant.
The melodrama made her laugh.
We talked about old times instead.
Things are more real here in the city.
One sentence follows another.
I make phone calls and feel important.
These fitful attempts are abandoned.
You shower and shave.
I read about my retirement benefits.

It's ten past ten.
It's five past one.
It's a quarter to three.
It's seven thirty.

She will listen to the news.
I felt my throat constrict.
At odd moments I would try to follow the flow backwards.

In a darkened theatre, I remembered my pleasure.
I thought of things I could do tomorrow.
She tries to help an old man who has fallen in the snow.
He is drunk and scowls at me.

They walked around the block several times, arm in arm.
They were singing old songs.
The veins in my hands are blue.

That day is drawing near.
Can you feel it?
I lost my suitcase at the train station.
It was full of presents for my daughter and her little girl.

Her juices must have been flowing.
She had had several cups of coffee.
She went outside for a breath of air.
She knew someone would fall like a domino.

You followed directions as best you could.
The sky glowed red on your left.
Everyone you passed was walking in the opposite direction.
Cars were turning on their headlights.

Several attempts at communication were made.
I receive a long distance call.
We have a foolish conversation.
We remember an underwater adventure we once shared.
She uses obscure words in our conversation.
After I hang up the phone, I look up words in the dictionary.
Threads of meaning are tied together.
I can breathe more easily.
I can relax and enjoy a beer.

I send long distance letters to my brother.
His home in the north is unchanging.
He watches the animals from his picture window.
His son is learning to watch, too.

I went to the doctor's on Friday.
I read magazines while I waited my turn.
She put her hands on my body.
She said that I was in good health.
I paid her with dollar bills that were old and soft.

It is a busy street.
She waited for the light to turn red.
She ambled along, window shopping.
Disco music comes out of the shops.
Someone grabs her from behind.
She whirls around.
Her teeth are bared.
It is her dear friend.
She laughs at the joke and they embrace in Spanish.

When we're parents let's spoil our children.
Let's give them everything.
Let's stand up for them when they act obnoxious.
Let's yell at the other kids when they beat up on our kid.
Let's hold them close.

My brother is proud of his son.
This seems like a good idea.
His perceptions are becoming sharper.
He eats his vegetables and says, "goo-goo."

So, this was shortly after we went to Buffalo.
We bought food and we sat on the porch.
You swam in the river; the Lordly Hudson River.
They talked about Chicago.
We've received several postcards from them this winter.
"You guys over the bad weather yet?"

I thought this tragedy would soften her.
Instead she is more disagreeable than ever.

The cold stung my cheeks.
Now I see she has begun to wear make-up.
Let me out here.
I'll get out on this corner.
Let's murder this girl.
We'll stab her with a knife.

"You won't be back," they said.
"I'll be back."
"You won't be back.
You won't be back."
No one was alarmed.
No one asked why.

Sunset proved to be the most auspicious hour for time travel.
The mind is in a particularly unstable condition just before
    dark.
One is more conscious of the grandness of physical phenomena
    during that half hour or so.

* * *

She huddles under a red blanket.
Things have changed.
She often goes hungry.
She allows herself to be abused.
She gazes for hours at crossroads.
I hear you bragging about your athletic ability.
You have a gleam in your eye.
Your cheeks are red as apples.
You'll notice different things from what I see.
I hear teenagers yelling to each other on the street.
They sing an old Beatles song.

Avoiding the drunk teenagers, I slipped into the supermarket.
The dazzling colors made my eyes pop.
I became giddy in the L-shaped produce department.
Nuts were across the aisle, processed meat in the center.
I bought pressed ham and red peppers.

It was unlike me.

In the morning I awoke.
I got dressed in the cold.
As I poured the coffee I glimpsed something.
I espied a monster from the corner of my eye.
It had shiny pointed teeth.
Its eyes were bleeding.
A putrid odor came from its fur.
It snarled at me.
My teeth were chattering.

Late at night, sobs awaken you.
It must be your neighbor upstairs.
You put your head under the pillow.
Tomorrow you will buy fresh fruit.

The wind blows from the south.
I was heading north.
The going was easy.
The wind pushed me along.

Dear Baba, I received your letter.
It was so good to hear from you.
I'm flattered by your attention.
The sweater will fit by next winter.
She looks so lovely in red.
Thank you so much.

Your neighbor greets you as you open the door.
Her cheeks are red from the cold.
You stumble a salutation.
She seems to have no cares.

I became my best friend, Baba.
I'm not kidding.
I really did.

There's a corner in New York where several streets come
    together at angles that are not ninety degrees.
My wife wants to get out of the city.
She really does.
She's going crazy.
We became each other.
What made you think you were becoming me?

I went to the bathroom.
A woman in red was washing her hands.
A girl at the mirror was putting on make-up and perfume.
The Muzak was playing fiercely.
I went into a cubicle and shut the door.

We all were gathered around the machines.
I don't know where she got the idea that Captain Hook could
    read her mind.

She met her husband when they were both cops.
She always had her head in a book.
She was thinking about going to law school.

Now they are married.
They disagree about everything.
He's a conservative and she's a liberal.
He says, "You don't believe in capital punishment but you
    believe in abortion."
She says, "That's after the fact."
They have a lively marriage.

My brother mails me photographs.
He talks about the cold weather.

You were cooking beans in your little trailer.
Night had fallen.
Animals made soft sounds in the Texas night.
You've fallen asleep in your chair.
My letter slips from your hand.

32

You scratch the dog in your sleep.
The radio plays only static.
Time has passed.
I'm watching television.
I'm sucking my fingers.
Ach! Vegetables have been long forgotten.
Meat is the order of the day.
There is no time for romance.
Ten year old memories come alive.
Her old friends have joined the CIA.
Can you believe this?

Red leaves fluttered down around you.
You suppressed your jealousy.
You looked down at a chair factory from a mountaintop.
You fingered the gold chain around your neck.

I'm relaxing.
I'm riding on a train.
I have no obligations.
I can think of what I want to.
Something fantastic was about to happen.
She left in a hurry.
She may have forgotten to lock the door.
She left her red sweater on the bed.
She may have missed her plane.

Out the window, rows of two-family houses are seen from above.
The cars look like toys.
Someone you know may be riding in one of them.

I will be home at 3:30.
At 4:00 I will take a red pill.
She will become invisible.
The sun will set.

A Martian landed on my doorstep.
It referred to the twentieth century.

Lonely Horse had us both up for tea.
We tried to explain to the Martians about the 1980s.
Galaxies spun around us.
I felt giddy.
O, I looked down at the blackness.
I thought of friends I was relieved to leave behind.
We stopped at a familiar station.
They played Little Anthony and the Imperials.
We traveled through the space station in an electric Buick.
Crazy Eddy is crazier than ever.
I yawned.

She's planning to go to the snack bar.
She thinks she'll go to the bar car.
I cannot restrain her.
Flock after flock of birds fly by.
I think it is a film loop.
The next stop is Providence.
The sky is bright.
Blanket statements are always refutable.

You learn to be a good girl from a song your father sings.
On an expense account anything is possible.
You can pick out the shiniest vegetables.
The newspaper confuses some of the facts.

I live to a ripe old age.
I take an apartment overlooking the river.
I perform heinous crimes in the dead of night.
I pull threads together for relatives.

You are relieved of decisions.
I whisk you through the night.
I'm a teenager but I know my way around.
A red blinking stoplight is a warning.
You are foolish to try and make plans with me.
I don't live like that.

* * *

They say they will but they never do.
Now all your ambitions crumble into dust.
Now your ideas seem foolish.

Now it's left to me to go to the market.
I'll go to the meat counter.
I'll dress you in your red sweater.
I dreamed I got a letter.

"Dear Chris, Thanks so much for your package which arrived
    today.
I'll while away the hours with it.
I'll play the shakahati flute.
I carry it on my shoulders.
It will fit her next winter."

I'm lonely without you.
I gaze at your picture every night.
I dance down the aisles.
I play your favorite song.
Tears drip down my face.
It's my favorite emotion.
I've been remembering the past.
Certain corners we took together.
Musical instruments make up the difference.
Feeling a distance you won't even acknowledge.

I've learned to be so good.
You're good for me.
You've squashed me.

There's a break in the Steak House murders in Oklahoma City.
Ironically the murders all took place last July.
A child was killed at the border.
American tourists were unable to go into the country.
Rivers have overflowed and the huge ice floes rushing down-

stream make sound like bombs.

The Islanders are 4 games behind the Canadiennes.
The Mets opened their season with a 4-3 win over St. Louis.

I've worked hard all day.
I've addressed serious questions.
The Mother of Me says to the Baby of Me, "You've worked hard
all day. What would you like for dinner?"
I stroll into the supermarket, gleeful.
I glide up and down the aisles humming with the Muzack.
I had heard that a new tense had been invented.
The apples were bruised, the lettuce wilted, the carrots
rubbery.
I suspected that it might describe the memories of what
would be.

JENNY HOLZER
EATING FRIENDS

TOP STORIES #7

EATING
FRIENDS

$2.00

EATING FRIENDS

A LITTLE GIRL HAD BEEN IN A COMA FOR WEEKS BUT SMILED AND CAME OUT OF IT WHEN THEY SANG SONGS.

CHILDHOOD WAS THE TIME FOR EXPERIMENTATION. THEY FOLDED WASHCLOTHS ON THEIR LEGS AND POURED SCALDING WATER ON THEM, ALWAYS STOPPING SHORT OF EXTREME RAIN AND VISIBLE BURNS.

HANDS-ON SOCIALIZATION PROMOTES HAPPY INTERPERSONAL RELATIONS. THE DESIRE FOR AND THE DEPENDENCE UPON FONDLING ENSURE THEIR REPEATED ATTEMPTS TO OBTAIN CARESSES AND THEIR WILLINGNESS TO RECIPROCATE.

HOW NICE TO SUPPLY THE NECESSARY COMFORTS. NUTRI-
ENTS AND LESSONS SO THAT THE OPTIMAL NUMBER OF
THEM GROW TO MATURITY AND ENJOY IT.

I SAW THEIR STUNNING BODIES GO SLACK AND GET HAIR IN
THE WRONG PLACES AND I VOWED I WOULD NOT PERMIT
THAT TO HAPPEN TO ME.

IF THE HOUSE IS BITTER COLD, ALL THE FLUIDS THEREIN, IF NOT
FROZEN, ARE STIFF AND SLOW.

IT CAN BE HELPFUL TO THINK OF THEM EATING THEIR FAVOR-
ITE FOODS AND OCCASIONALLY THROWING UP AND GET-
TING BITS STUCK IN THEIR NOSES.

IT CAN BE STARTLING TO SEE THEIR BREATH, LET ALONE THE
BREATHING OF A CROWD. YOU USUALLY DON'T BELIEVE
THAT THEY EXTEND THAT FAR.

IT IS UNFAIR TO TEAR THEM APART WHEN THEIR HEALTH AND
EXUBERANCE THREATEN YOU.

IT MAKES A DIFFERENCE IF YOU'RE INTIMATE WITH THEM, IF
YOU'RE DEPENDENT UPON THEM. THEY WILL ONLY TOLERATE
OR SUPPORT CERTAIN ACTIONS AND THIS INFLUENCES
WHAT YOU BELIEVE TO BE POSSIBLE OR DESIRABLE.

IT'S AN ODD FEELING WHEN YOU TRIGGER INSTINCTIVE BE-HAVIOR—LIKE NURSING—IN THEM. IT'S FUNNY TO BE IN THEIR PRESENCE WHILE A DIFFERENT PART OF THE NERVOUS SYSTEM TAKES OVER AND THEIR EYES GET STRANGE.

IT'S AWFUL TO SEE THEM DEFORMED BECAUSE THEY ARE RIG-ID WITH FEAR.

IT'S EASY FOR THEM TO FEEL BETRAYED WHEN THEY'RE JUST WAVING THEIR ARMS AROUND AND THEY COME CRASHING DOWN ON A SHARP OBJECT.

IT'S NICE WHEN THEY DECIDE THEY LIKE SOMEONE, AND WITHOUT DECLARING THEMSELVES, DO WHAT'S POSSIBLE TO FURTHER THEIR HAPPINESS. THIS CAN TAKE THE FORM OF GIFTS, LOVELY FOOD, PUBLICITY, ADVANCE WARNING OR EASY MOBILITY.

MORE THAN ONCE THEY'VE WAXENED WITH TEARS RUN-NING DOWN THEIR CHEEKS. THEY HAVE HAD TO THINK WHETHER THEY WERE CRYING OR WHETHER IT WAS INVOL-UNTARY LIKE DROOLING.

SOMEONE WANTS TO CUT A HOLE IN YOU AND FUCK YOU THROUGH IT, BUDDY.

THE MOUTH IS INTERESTING BECAUSE IT'S ONE OF THOSE PLACES WHERE THE DRY OUTSIDE MOVES TOWARD THE SLIPPERY INSIDE.

THE SMALLEST THING CAN MAKE THEM SEXUALLY UNAPPEALING. A MISPLACED MOLE OR A PARTICULAR HAIR PATTERN CAN DO IT. THERE'S NO REASON FOR THIS, BUT IT'S JUST AS WELL.

THERE'S NO REASON TO SLEEP CURLED UP AND BENT. IT'S NOT COMFORTABLE, IT'S NOT GOOD FOR THEM AND IT DOESN'T PROTECT THEM FROM DANGER. IF THEY'RE WORRIED ABOUT AN ATTACK THEY SHOULD STAY AWAKE OR SLEEP LIGHTLY WITH LIMBS UNFURLED FOR ACTION.

THERE'S THE SENSATION OF A LOT OF FLESH WHEN EVERY SINGLE HAIR STANDS UP. THIS HAPPENS WHEN THEY ARE COLD AND NAKED, AROUSED OR SIMPLY TERRIFIED.

THEY LIKE TO NIBBLE ON THE INSIDE OF THEIR OWN CHEEKS. I'VE SEEN AN OTHERWISE LOVELY GIRL CONTORT HER FACE TO REACH A FAVORITE SPOT. THEY HAVE BITE LINES WHERE REPEATED NIPS HAVE BUILT UP A RIDGE OF SCAR TISSUE.

THEY RARELY FOLLOW MOTION WITH THEIR EYES IF THEIR HEADS ARE UPSIDE DOWN. THEY RAISE THEIR HEADS TO AN UPRIGHT ORIENTATION TO WATCH WHAT GOES ON AROUND THEM. DOES THIS DENOTE A LACK OF CONFIDENCE IN THEIR ABILITY TO REACT WHEN SUPINE?

THEY SHOULD LIMIT THE NUMBER OF TIMES THEY ACT AGAINST THEIR NATURE, LIKE SLEEPING WITH PEOPLE THEY HATE. IT'S ALL RIGHT TO TEST THEIR CAPABILITIES, BUT IF THEY DON'T KNOW WHEN TO STOP, THEY'LL HURT THEMSELVES.

THEY WERE STRIPPING A THIRD FELLOW SO THAT IN A MATTER OF SECONDS HE LAY CURLED-UP AND NAKED ON THE SIDEWALK.

TWO CREATURES CAN WANT TO MOVE AND REST IN CLOSE PROXIMITY EVEN IF THEY ARE AFRAID OF EACH OTHER. I'M THINKING OF A WILD ANIMAL FOLLOWING ONE OF THEM IN THE WOODS.

USUALLY YOU COME OUT WITH STUFF ON YOU WHEN YOU'VE BEEN IN THEIR THOUGHTS OR BODIES.

WHEN YOU'RE ON THE VERGE OF DECIDING THAT YOU DON'T LIKE THEM, IT'S AWFUL WHEN THEY SMILE AND THEIR TEETH LOOK ABSOLUTELY EVEN AND FALSE.

WITH BLEEDING INSIDE THE HEAD THERE IS A METALLIC TASTE AT THE BACK OF THE THROAT.

YOU CAN WATCH THEM ALIGN THEMSELVES WHEN TROUBLE IS IN THE AIR. SOME PREFER TO BE CLOSE TO THOSE AT THE TOP, AND OTHERS WANT TO BE CLOSE TO THOSE AT THE BOTTOM. IT'S A QUESTION OF WHO FRIGHTENS THEM MORE AND WHO THEY WANT TO BE LIKE.

TOP STORIES #9

$2.50

NEW YORK CITY IN 1979

by Kathy Acker

KATHY ACKER

NEW YORK CITY IN 1979

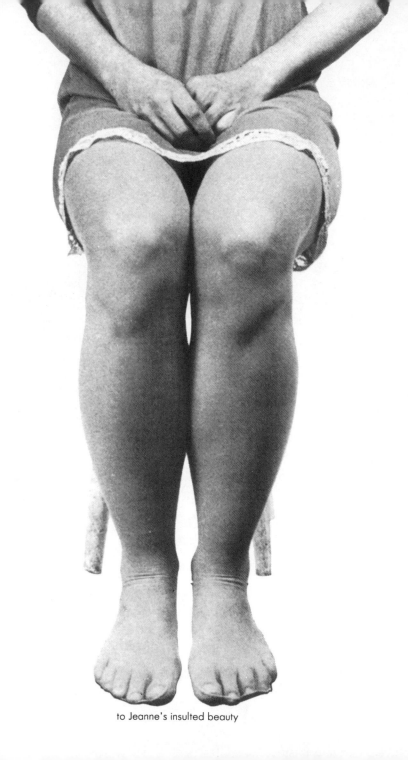

to Jeanne's insulted beauty

SOME people say New York City is evil and they wouldn't live there for all the money in the world.

These are the same people who elected Johnson, Nixon, Carter President and Koch Mayor of New York.

THE WHORES IN JAIL AT NIGHT

—Well, my man's gonna get me out of here as soon as he can.

—When's that gonna be, honey?

—So what? Your man pays so he can put you back on the street as soon as possible.

—Well, what if he want me back on the street? That's where I belong. I make him good money, don't I? He knows that I'm a good girl.

—Your man ain't anything! Johnny says that if I don't work my ass off for him, he's not going to let me back in the house.

—I have to earn two hundred before I can go back.

—Two hundred? That ain't shit! You can earn two hundred in less than a night. I have to earn four hundred or I might just as well forget sleeping, and there's no running away from Him. My baby is the toughest there is.

—Well, shit girl, if I don't come back with eight hundred I get my ass whupped off.

—That's cause you're junk.

—I ain't no stiff! All of you are junkies. I know what you do!

—What's the matter, honey?

—You've been sitting on that thing for an hour.

—The pains are getting bad. OOgh. I've been bleeding two days now.

—OOgh OOgh OOgh.

—She's gonna bang her head off. She needs a shot.

—Tie a sweater around her head. She's gonna break her head open.

—You should see a doctor, honey.

—The doctor told me I'm having an abortion.

—Matron, Goddamnit. Get your ass over here matron!

—I haven't been bleeding this bad. Maybe this is the real abortion.

—Matron! This little girl is having an abortion! You do something. Where the hell is that asshole woman? (The matron throws an open piece of Kotex to the girl.) The service here is getting worse and worse!

—You're not in a hotel, honey.

49

—It used to be better than this. There's not even any goddamn food. This place is definitely going downhill.

—Oh, shutup. I'm trying to sleep. I need my sleep, unlike you girls, cause I'm going back to work tomorrow.

—Now what the hell do you need sleep for? This is a party. You sleep on your job.

—I sure know this is the only time I get any rest. Tomorrow it's back on the street again.

—If we're lucky.

LESBIANS are women who prefer their own ways to male ways.

LESBIANS prefer the convoluting halls of sensuality to direct goal-pursuing mores.

LESBIANS have made a small world deep within and separated from the world. What has usually been called the world is the male world.

Convoluting halls of sensuality lead to depend on illusions. Lies and silence are realer than truth.

Either you're in love with someone or you're not. The one thing about being in love with someone is you know you're in love: You're either flying or you're about to kill yourself.

I don't know anyone I'm in love with or I don't know if I'm in love. I have all these memories. I remember that as soon as I've gotten fucked, like a dog I no longer care about the man who just fucked me who I was madly in love with.

So why should I spend a hundred dollars to fly to Toronto to get laid by someone I don't know if I love I don't know if I can love I'm an abortion? I mean a hundred dollars and once I get laid I'll be in agony: I won't be doing exactly what I want. I can't live normally i.e. with love so: there is no more life.

The world is gray afterbirth. Fake. All of New York City is fake is going to go all my friends are going crazy all my friends know they're going crazy disaster is the only thing that's happening.

Suddenly these outbursts in the fake, cause they're so open, spawn a new growth. I'm waiting to see this growth.

I want more and more horrible disaster in New York cause I desperately want to see that new thing that is going to happen this year.

JANEY is a woman who has sexually hurt and been sexually hurt so much she's now frigid.

She doesn't want to see her husband anymore. There's nothing between them.

Her husband agrees with her that there's nothing more between them.

But there's no such thing as nothingness. Not here. Only death whatever that is is nothing. All the ways people are talking to her now mean nothing. She doesn't want to speak words that are meaningless.

Janey doesn't want to see her husband again.

The quality of life in this city stinks. Is almost nothing. Most people now are deaf-mutes only inside they're screaming. BLOOD. A lot of blood inside is going to fall. MORE and MORE because inside is outside.

New York City will become alive again when the people begin to speak to each other again not information but real emotion. A grave is spreading its legs and BEGGING FOR LOVE.

Robert, Janey's husband, is almost a zombie.

He walks talks plays his saxophone pays for groceries almost like every other human. There's no past. The last six years didn't exist. Janey hates him. He made her a hole. He blasted into her. He has no feeling. The light blue eyes he gave her; the gentle hands; the adoration: AREN'T. NO CRIME. NO BLOOD. THE NEW CITY. Like in Fritz Lang's METROPOLIS.

This year suffering has so blasted all feelings out of her she's become a person. Janey believes it's necessary to blast open her mind constantly and destroy EVERY PARTICLE OF MEMORY THAT SHE LIKES.

A sleeveless black T-shirt binds Janey's breasts. Pleated black fake-leather pants hide her cocklessness. A thin leopard tie winds around her neck. One gold-plated watch, the only remembrance of the dead mother, binds one wrist. A thin black leather band binds the other. The head is almost shaved. Two round prescription mirrors mask the eyes.

Johnny is a man who don't want to be living so he doesn't appear to be a man. All his life everyone wanted him to be something. His Jewish mother wanted him to be famous so he wouldn't live the life she was living. The two main girlfriends he has had wanted him to support them in the manner to which they certainly weren't accustomed even though he couldn't put his flabby hands on a penny. His father wanted him to shut up.

All Johnny wants to do is make music. He wants to keep everyone and everything who takes him away from his music off him. Since he can't afford human contact, he can't afford desire. Therefore he hangs around with rich zombies who never have anything to do with feelings. This is a typical New York artist attitude.

New York City is a pit-hole: Since the United States government, having decided that New York City is no longer part of the United States of America, is dumping all the laws the rich people want such as anti-rent-control laws and all the people they don't want (artists, poor minorities, and the media in general) on the city and refusing the city Federal funds; the American bourgeoisie has left. Only the poor: artists, Puerto Ricans who can't afford to move . . . and rich Europeans who fleeing the terrorists don't give a shit about New York . . . inhabit this city.

Meanwhile the temperature is getting hotter and hotter so no one can think clearly. No one perceives. No one cares. Insane madness come out like life is a terrific party.

IN FRONT OF THE MUDD CLUB, 77 WHITE STREET

Two rich couples drop out of a limousine. The women are wearing outfits the poor people who were in ten years ago wore ten years ago. The men are just neutral. All the poor people who're making this club fashionable so the rich want to hang out here, even though the poor still never make a buck off the rich pleasure, are sitting on cars, watching the rich people walk up to the club.

Some creeps around the club's entrance. An open-shirted skinny guy who says he's just an artist is choosing who he'll let into the club. Since it's 3:30 A.M. there aren't many creeps. The artist won't let the rich hippies into the club.

—Look at that car.

—Jesus. It's those rich hippies' car.

—Let's take it.

—That's the chauffeur over there.

—Let's kidnap him.

—Let's knock him over the head with a bottle.

—I don't want no terrorism. I wanna go for a ride.

—That's right. We've got nothing to do with terrorism. We'll just explain we want to borrow the car for an hour.

—Maybe he'll lend us the car if we explain we're terrorists-in-training. We want to use that car to try out terrorist tricks.

After 45 minutes the rich people climb back into their limousine and their chauffeur drives them away.

A girl who has gobs of brown hair like the foam on a cappuccino in Little Italy, black patent leather S&M heels, two unfashionable tits stuffed into a pale green corset, and extremely fashionable black fake leather tights heaves her large self off a car top. She's holding an empty bottle.

Diego senses there's going to be trouble. He gets off his car top. Is walking slowly towards the girl.

The bottle keeps waving. Finally the girl finds some courage heaves the bottle at the skinny entrance artist.

The girl and the artist battle it out up the street. Some of the people who are sitting on cars separate them. We see the girl throw herself back on a car top. Her tits are bouncing so hard she must want our attention and she's getting insecure, maybe violent, cause she isn't getting enough. Better give us a better show. She sticks her middle finger into the air as far as she can. She writhes around on the top of the car. Her movements are so spasmatic she must be nuts.

A yellow taxi cab is slowly making its way to the club. On one side of this taxi cab's the club entrance. The other side is the girl writ(h)ing away on the black car. Three girls who are pretending to be transvestites are lifting themselves out of the cab elegantly around the big girl's body. The first body is encased into a translucent white girdle. A series of diagonal panels leads directly to her cunt. The other two dresses are tight and white. They are wriggling their way toward the club. The big girl, whom the taxi driver refused to let in his cab, wriggling because she's been rejected but not wriggling as much, is bumping into them. They're tottering away from her because she has syphilis.

Now the big girl is unsuccessfully trying to climb through a private white car's window now she's running hips hooking even faster into an alleyway taxi whose driver is locking his doors and windows against her. She's offering him a blow-job. Now an ugly boy with a huge safety pin stuck through his upper lip, walking up and down the street, is shooting at us with his watergun.

The dyke sitting next to me is saying earlier in the evening she pulled at this safety pin.

It's four o'clock A.M. It's still too hot. Wet heat's squeezing this city. The air's mist. The liquid's that seeping out of human flesh pores is gonna harden into a smooth shiny shell so we're going to become reptiles.

No one wants to move anymore. No one wants to be in a body Physical possessions can go to hell even in this night.

Johnny like all other New York inhabitants doesn't want anything to do with sex. He hates sex because the air's hot, because feelings are dull, and because humans are repulsive.

Like all the other New Yorker's he's telling females he's strictly gay and males all faggots ought to burn in hell and they are. He's doing this because when he was sixteen years old his parents who wanted him to die stuck him in the Merchant Marines and all the marines cause this is what they do raped his ass off with many doses of coke.

Baudelaire doesn't go directly toward self-satisfaction cause of the following mechanism: X wants Y and, for whatever reasons, thinks it shouldn't want Y. X thinks it is BAD because it wants Y. What X wants is Y and to be GOOD.

Baudelaire does the following to solve this dilemma: He understands that some agency (his parents, society, his mistress, etc.) is saying that wanting Y is BAD. This agency is authority is right. The authority will punish him because he's BAD. The authority will punish him as much as possible, punish me punish me, more than is necessary till it has to be obvious to everyone that the punishment is unjust. Punishers are unjust. All authority right now stinks to high hell. Therefore there is no GOOD and BAD. X cannot be BAD.

It's necessary to go to as many extremes as possible.

As soon as Johnny sees Janey he wants to have sex with her. Johnny takes out his cock and rubs it. He walks over to Janey, puts his arms around her shoulders so he's pinning her against a concrete wall.

Johnny says, "You're always talking about sex. Are you going to spread your legs for me like you spread your legs all the time for any guy you don't know?"

Janey replies, "I'm not fucking anymore cause sex is a prison. It's become a support of this post-capitalist system like art. Businessmen who want to make money have to turn up a product that people'll buy and want to keep buying. Since American consumers now own every object there is plus they don't have any money anyway cause they're being squeezed between inflation and depression, just like fucking, these businessmen have to discover products that obvious necessity sells. Sex is such a product. Just get rid of the puritanism sweetheart your parents spoonfed you in between materialism which the sexual revolution did thanks to free love and hippies sex is a terrific hook. Sexual desire is a naturally fluctuating phenomena. The sex product presents a naturally expanding market. Now capitalists are doing everything they can to bring world sexual desire to an unbearable edge.

"I don't want to be hurt again. Getting hurt or rejected is more dangerous than I know because now everytime I get sexually rejected I get dangerously physically sick. I don't want to hurt again. Everytime I hurt I feel so disgusted with myself—that by following some stupid body desire I didn't HAVE to follow, I killed the tender nerves of someone else. I retreat into myself. I again become frigid."

"I never have fun."

Johnny says, "You want to be as desperate as possible but you don't have to be desperate. You're going to be a success. Everybody knows you're going to be a success. Wouldn't you like to give up this artistic life which you know isn't rewarding cause artists now have to turn their work/selves into marketable objects/fluctuating images/fashion have to competitively knife each other in the back because we're not people, can't treat each other like people, no feelings, loneliness comes from the world of rationality, robots, everything one as objects defined separate from each other? The whole impetus for art in the first place is gone bye-bye? You know you want to get away from this media world."

Janey replies, "I don't know what I want now. I know the New York City world is more complex and desirable even though everything you're saying's true. I don't know what my heart is cause I'm corrupted."

"Become pure again. Love. You have to will. You can do what you will. Then love'll enter your heart."

"I'm not capable of loving anyone. I'm a freak. Love's an obsession that only weird people have. I'm going to be a robot for the rest of my life. This is confusing to be a human being, but robotism is what's present."

"It's unnatural to be sexless. You eat alone and that's freaky."

"I am lonely out of my mind. I am miserable out of my mind. Open open what are you touching me. Touching me. Now I'm going into the state where desire comes out like a monster. Sex I love you. I'll do anything to touch you. I've got to fuck. Don't you understand don't you have needs as much as I have needs DON'T YOU HAVE TO GET LAID?"

—Janey, close that door. What's the matter with you? Why aren't you doing what I tell you?

—I'll do whatever you tell me, nana.

—That's right. Now go into that drawer and get that check-book for me. The Chase Manhattan one, not the other one. Give me both of them. I'll show you which one.

—I can find it, nana. No, it's not this one.

—Give me both of them. I'll do it.

—Here you are, nana. This is the one you want, isn't it?

—Now sit yourself down and write yourself out a check for $10,000. It doesn't matter which check you write it on

—Ten thousand dollars! Are you sure about this, nana?

—Do what I tell you. Write yourself out a check for ten thousand dollars.

—Uh O.K. What's the date?

—It doesn't matter. Put any date you want. Now hand me my glasses. They're over there.

—I'm just going to clean them. They're dirty.

—You can clean them for me later. Give them to me.

—Are . . . you sure you want to do this?

—Now I'm going to tell you something, Janey. Invest this. Buy yourself 100 shares of AT&T. You can fritter it away if you want. Good riddance to you. If your mother had invested the 800 shares of IBM I gave her, she would have had a steady income and wouldn't have had to commit suicide. Well, she needed the money. If you invest in AT&T, you'll always have an income.

—I don't know what to say. I've never seen so much money before. I've never seen so much money before.

—You do what I tell you to. Buy AT&T.

—I'll put the money in a bank, nana, and as soon as it clears I'll buy AT&T.

At ten o'clock the next morning Nana is still asleep. A rich salesman who was spending his winter in New York had in-stalled her in a huge apartment on Park Avenue for six months. The apartment's rooms are tremendous, too big for her tiny body, and are still partly unfurnished. Thick silk daybed spreads ivory-handled white feather fans hanging above contrast the black-and-red "naturalistic" clown portraits in the "study" that give an air of culture rather than of call-girl. A call-girl or mis-tress, as soon as her first man is gone, is no longer innocent. No one to help her, constantly harassed by rent and food bills, in need of elegant clothing and cosmetics to keep surviving, she has to use her sex to get money.

Nana's sleeping on her stomach, her bare arms hugging instead of a man a pillow into which she's buried a face soft with sleep. The bedroom and the small adjoining dressingroom are the only two properly furnished rooms. A ray of light filtered through the gray richly-laced curtain focuses a rosewood bedstead covered by carved Chinese figures, the bedstead covered by white linen sheets; covered by a pale blue silk quilt; covered by a pale white silk quilt; Chinese pictures composed of five to seven layers of carved ivory, almost sculptures rather than pictures, surround these gleaming layers.

She feels around and, finding no one, calls her maid.

"Paul left ten minutes ago," the girl says as she walks into the room. "He didn't want to wake you. I asked him if he wanted coffee but he said he was in a rush. He'll see you his usual time tomorrow."

"Tomorrow tomorrow," the prostitute can never get anything straight, "can he come tomorrow?"

"Wednesday's Paul's day. Today you see the furrier."

"I remember," she says, sitting up, "the old furrier told me he's coming Wednesday and I can't go against him. Paul'll have to come another day."

"You didn't tell me. If you don't tell me what's going on, I'm going to get things confused and your Johns'll be running into each other!"

Nana stretches her fatty arms over her head and yawns. Two bunches of short brown hairs are sticking out of her armpits. "I'll call Paul and tell him to come back tonight. No. I won't sleep with anyone tonight. Can I afford it? I'll tell Paul to come on Tuesday's after this and I'll have tonight to myself!" Her nightgown slips down her nipples surrounded by one long brown hair and the rest of her hair, loose and tousled, flows over her still-wet sheets.

Bet—I think feminism is the only thing that matters.

Janey (yawning)—I'm so tired all I can do is sleep all day

(only she doesn't fall asleep cause she's suddenly attracted to Michael who's like every other guy she's attracted to married to a friend of hers.)

Bet—First of all feminism is only possible in a socialist state.

Janey—But Russia stinks as much as the United States these days. What has this got to do with your film?

Bet—Cause feminism depends of four factors: First of all, women have to have economic independence. If they don't have that they don't have anything. Second, free daycare centers. Abortions, (counting on her fingers). Fourth, decent housing.

Janey—I mean those are just material considerations. You're accepting the materialism this society teaches. I mean look I've had lots of abortions I can fuck anyone I want—well, I could— I'm still in prison. I'm not talking about myself.

Bet—Are you against abortions?

Janey—How could I be against abortions? I've had fucking five of them. I can't be against abortions. I just think all that stuff is back in the 1920's. It doesn't apply to this world. This world is different than all that socialism: those multi-national corporations control everything.

Louie—You just don't know how things are cause the feminist movement here is nothing compared to the feminist movements in Italy, England, and Australia. That's where women really stick together.

Janey—That's not true! Feminism here, sure it's not the old feminism the groups Gloria Steinem and Ti-Grace, but they were *so* straight. It's much better now: it's just underground it's not so public.

Louie—The only women in Abercrombie's and Fitch's films are those traditionally male defined types.

The women are always whores or bitches. They have no power.

Janey—Women are whores now. I think women every time they fuck no matter who they fuck should get paid. When they fuck their boyfriends their husbands. That's the way things are only the women don't get paid.

Louie—Look at Carter's films. There are no women's roles. The only two women in the film who aren't bit players are France who's a bitch and England who's a whore.

Janey—But that's how things were in Rome of that time.

Bet—But, Jane, we're saying things have to be different. Our friends can't keep upholding the sexist state of women in their work.

Janey—You know about Abercrombie and Fitch. I don't even bother saying anything to them. But Carter's film: you've got to look at why an artist does what he does. Otherwise you're you're not being fair. In ROME Carter's saying the decadent Roman society was like this one.

Louie—The one that a certain small group of artists in New York lives in.

Janey—Yeah.

Louie—He's saying the men we know treat women only as whores and bitches.

Janey—So what are you complaining about?

Bet—Before you were saying you have no one to talk to about your work. That's what I'm saying. We've got to tell Abercrombie and Fitch what they're doing. We've got to start portraying women as strong showing women as the power of this society.

Janey—But we're not.

Bet—But how else are we going to be? In Italy there was this women's art festival. A friend of ours who does performance dressed as a woman and did a performance. Then he revealed he was a man. The women in the festival beat him up and called the police.

Michael—The police?

Janey—Was he good?

Bet—He was the best performer there.

Louie—I think calling the police is weird. They should have just beaten him up.

Janey—I don't like the police.

I WANT ALL THE ABOVE TO BE THE SUN

INTENSE SEXUAL DESIRE IS THE GREATEST THING
IN THE WORLD

Janey dreams of cocks. Janey sees cocks instead of objects.
Janey has to fuck.

This is the way Sex drives Janey crazy: Before Janey fucks, she
keeps her wants in cells. As soon as Janey's fucking she wants to
be adored as much as possible at the same time as, its other extreme, ignored as much as possible. More than this: Janey can no
longer perceive herself wanting. Janey is Want.

It's worse than this: If Janey gets sexually rejected her body
becomes sick. If she doesn't get who she wants she naturally
revolts.

This is the nature of reality. No rationality possible. Only this
is true. The world in which there is no feeling, the robot world,
doesn't exist. This world is a very dangerous place to live in.

Old women just cause they're old and no man'll fuck them
don't stop wanting sex.

The old actress isn't good anymore. But she keeps on acting
even though she knows all the audiences mock her hideousness
and lack of context cause she adores acting. Her legs are gro-
tesque: FLABBY. Above, hidden within the folds of skin, there's
an ugly cunt. Two long flaps of white thin speckled by black
hairs like a pig's cock flesh hang down to the knees. There's no
feeling in them. Between these two flaps of skin the meat is red
folds and drips a white slime that poisons what ever it touches.
Just one drop burns a hole into anything. An odor of garbage in-
fested by maggots floats out of this cunt. One wants to vomit.
The meat is so red it looks like someone hacked a body to bits
with a cleaver or like the bright red lines under the purple lines
on the translucent skin of a woman's body found dead three days
ago. This red leads to a hole, a hole of redness, round and round,
black nausea. The old actress is black nausea because she reminds us of death. Yet she keeps plying her trade and that makes
her trade weird. Glory be to those humans who are absolutely
NOTHING for the opinions of other humans: they are the true
owners of illusions, transformations, and themselves.

Old people are supposed to be smarter than young people.

Old people in this country the United States of America are treated like total shit. Since most people spend their lives mentally dwelling on the material, they have no mental freedom, when they grow old and their skin rots and their bodies turn to putrefying sand and they can't do physical exercise and they can't indulge in bodily pleasure and they're all ugly anyway; suddenly they got nothing. Having nothing, you think they could at least be shut up in opiated dens so maybe they have a chance to develop dreams or at least they could warn their kids to do something else besides being materialistic. But the way this country's set up, there's not even opiated homes to hide this feelinglessness: old people have to go either to children's or most often into rest homes where they're shunted into wheelchairs and made as fast as possible into zombies cause it's easier to handle a zombie, if you have to handle anything, than a human. So an old person has a big empty hollow space with nothing in it, just ugh, and that's life: nothing else is going to happen, there's just ugh stop.

ANYTHING THAT DESTROYS LIMITS

Afterwards Janey and Johnny went to an all-night movie. All during the first movie Janey's sort of leaning against Johnny cause she's unsure he's attracted to her and she doesn't want to embarrass him (her) in case he ain't. She kinda scrunches against him. One point Johnny is pressing his knee against her knee but she still ain't sure.

Some Like It Hot ends. All the rest of the painters are gonna leave the movie house cause they've seen *The Misfits*. Separately Janey and Johnny say they're going to stay. The painters are walking out. The movie theatre is black.

Janey still doesn't know what Johnny's feelings are.

A third way through the second movie Johnny's hand grabs her knee. Her whole body becomes crazy. She puts her right hand into his hand but he doesn't want the hand.

Johnny's hand, rubbing her tan leg, is inching closer to her cunt. The hand is moving roughly, grabbing handfuls of flesh, the flesh and blood crawling. He's not responding to anything she's doing.

Finally she's tentatively touching his leg. His hand is pouncing on her right hand setting it an inch below his cock. Her body's becoming even crazier and she's more content.

His other hand is inching slower toward her open slimy hole. Cause the theatre is small, not very dark, and the seats aren't too steep, everyone sitting around them is watching exactly what they're doing. Her black dress is shoved up around her young thighs. His hand is almost curving around her dark-pantied cunt. Her and his legs are intertwined. Despite fear she's sure to be arrested just like in a porn book because fear she's wanting him to stick his cock up her right now.

His hand is roughly travelling around her cunt, never touching nothing, smaller and smaller circles.

Morning. The movie house lights go on. Johnny looks at Janey like she's a business acquaintance. From now on everything Janey does is for the purpose of getting Johnny's dick into her.

Johnny, "Let's get out of here."

New York City at six in the morning is beautiful. Empty streets except for a few bums. No garbage. A slight shudder of air down the long long streets. Pale gray prevails. Janey's going to kill

Johnny if he doesn't give her his cock instantaneously. She's thinking ways to get him to give her his cock. Her body becomes even crazier. Her body takes over. Turn on him. Throw arms around his neck. Back him against car. Shove clothed cunt against clothed cock. Lick ear because that's what there is.

Lick your ear.

Lick your ear.

Well?

I don't know.

What don't you know? You don't know if you want to?

Turn on him. Throw arms around his neck. Back him against car. Shove clothed cunt against clothed cock. Lick ear because that's what there is.

Obviously I want to.

I don't care what you do. You can come home with me; you can take a rain check; you cannot take a rain check.

I have to see my lawyer tomorrow. Then I have lunch with Ray.

Turn on him. Throw arms around his neck. Back him against car. Shove clothed cunt against clothed cock. Lick ear because that's what there is.

You're not helping me much.

You're not helping me much.

Through this morning they walk to her apartment. Johnny and Janey don't touch. Johnny and Janey don't talk to each other.

Johnny is saying that Janey's going to invite him up for a few minutes.

Janey is pouring Johnny a glass of Scotch. Janey is sitting in her bedroom on her bed. Johnny is untying the string holding up her black sheath. Johnny's saliva-wettened fingers are pinching her nipple. Johnny is lifting her body over his prostrate body. Johnny's making her cunt rub very roughly through the clothes against his huge cock. Johnny's taking her off him and lifting her dress over her body. Janey's saying, "Your cock is huge." Janey's placing her lips around Johnny's huge cock. Janey's easing her black underpants over her feet.

Johnny's moaning like he's about to come. Janey's lips are letting go his cock. Johnny's lifting Janey's body over his body so the top of his cock is just touching her lips. His hands on her thighs are pulling her down fast and hard. His cock is so huge it is entering her cunt painfully. His body is immediately moving quickly violently shudders. The cock is entering the bottom of Janey's cunt. Janey is coming. Johnny's hands are not holding Janey's thighs firmly enough and Johnny's moving too quickly to keep Janey coming. Johnny is building up to coming.

That's all right yes I that's all right. I'm coming again smooth of you oh smooth, goes on and on, am I coming am I not coming.

Janey's rolling off of Johnny. Johnny's pulling the black pants he's still wearing over his thighs because he has to go home. Janey's telling him she has to sleep alone even though she isn't knowing what she's feeling. At the door to Janey's apartment Johnny's telling Janey he's going to call her. Johnny walks out the door and doesn't see Janey again.

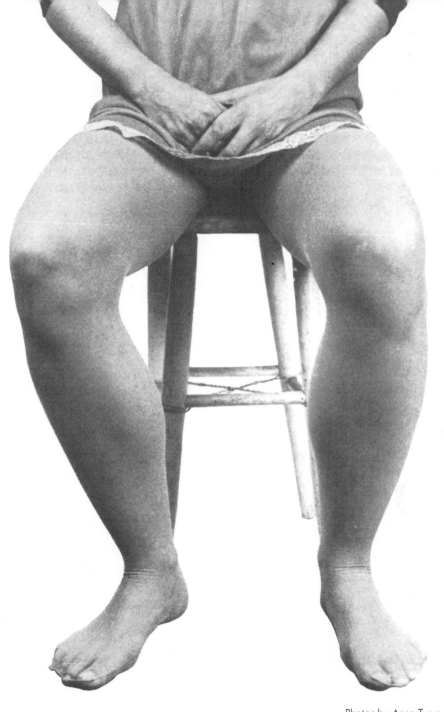

LYNNE TILLMAN & JANE DICKSON

LIVING WITH
CONTRADICTIONS

He didn't want to fight in any war and she didn't want to have a child. They had been living together for three years and still didn't have a way to refer to each other that didn't sound stupid, false, or antiquated. Language follows change and there wasn't any language to use.

Partners in a pairbonded situation; that sounded neutral. Of course living with someone isn't a neutral situation. Julie and Joe aren't cavedwellers. They don't live together as lovers or as husband and wife.

How long would this century be called modern or, even, post-modern? Perhaps relationships between people in the 14th century were more equitable, less fantastic. Not that Julie would've wanted to have been the miller's wife, or Joe, the miller.

In other centuries, different relationships. Less presumption, less intimacy? Before capitalism, early capitalism, no capitalism, feudalism. Feudal relationships. I want one of those, Julie thought, something feudal. What would it be like not to have a contemporary mind?

Intimacy is something people used to talk about before com-
mercials. Now there's nothing to say.

People are intimate with their analysts, if they're lucky. What could be more intimate than an advertisement for Ivory soap? It's impossible not to be affected.

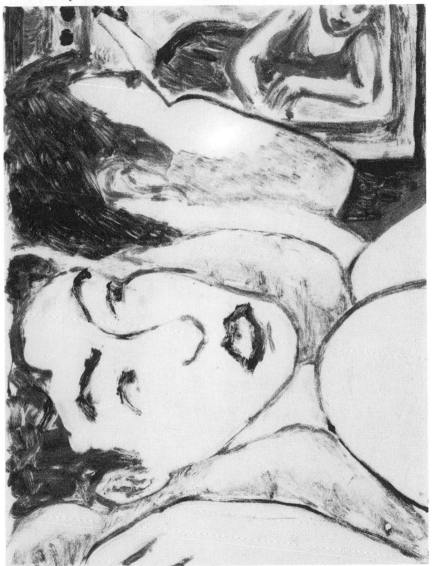

The manufacture of desire and the evidence of real desire. But "real" desire is for what—for what is real or manufactured?

Other people's passions always leave you cold. There is nothing like really being held. They didn't expect to be everything to each other.

The first year they lived together was a battle to be together and to be separate. A silent battle, because you can't fight the fight together, it defeats the purpose of the battle.

You can't talk about relationships, at least they didn't; they talked about things that happened and things that didn't. Daily life is very daily.

The great adventure, the pioneering thing, is to live together and not be a couple. The expectation is indefatigable and exhausting. Julie bought an Italian postcard, circa 1953, showing an ardent man and woman, locked in embrace. And looking at each other. Except that one of her eyes was roving out, the other in, and his eyes, looking at her, were crossed.

Like star-crossed lovers' eyes should be, she thought. She drew a triangle around their eyes, which made them still more distorted. People would ask, "Where's Joe?" as if there was something supposed to be attached to her. The attachment, my dear, isn't tangible, she wanted to say, but it is also physical.

New cars, new lovers. Sometimes she felt like Ma Kettle in a situation comedy, looked on from the outside. You're either on the inside looking out or the outside looking in. (Then there's the inside looking in, the outside looking out.)

Joe: We're old love.
Julie: We're familiar with each other.

Julie didn't mind except that she didn't have anyone new to talk about, the way her friends did. Consumerism in love. One friend told her that talking about the person you lived with was like airing your clean laundry in public.

Familiarity was, for her, better than romance. She'd been in love enough. Being in love is a fiction that lasts an hour and a half, feature-length, and then you're hungry again. Unromantic old love comforted her, like a room to read in.

Joe: You hooked up with me at the end of your hard-guy
       period.
Julie: How do you know?
Joe: I know.

So, Julie and Joe were just part of the great heterosexual capitalist family thrall, possessing each other.

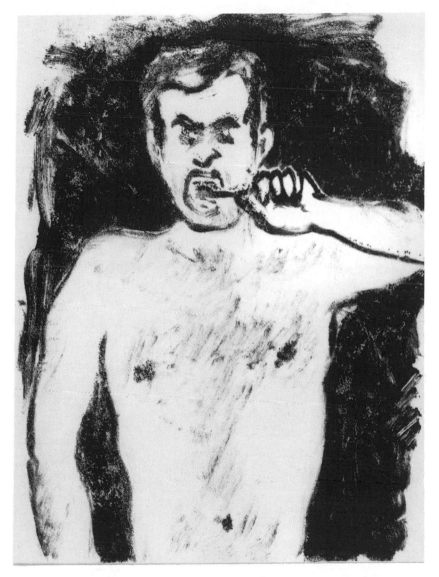

Contradictions make life finer. Ambivalence is just another word for love, becoming romantic about the unconscious.

Where does one find comfort, even constancy. To find it in an idea or in the flesh. We do incorporate ideas, after all.

You can accept the irrational over and again, you can renounce your feelings every day, but you're still a baby. An infant outside of reason, speaking reasonably about the unreasonable.

Calling love desire doesn't change the need. Julie couldn't abandon her desire for love. It was a pleasurable contradiction and it was against all reason.

JANET STEIN
SHATTERED ROMANCE

CONSTANCE DEJONG

I.T.I.L.O.E.

I.T.I.L.O.E.

FROM A NARROW BAND AT THE END OF THE RADIO DIAL

"Midnight, September 26, 1980"

"The Night of the Last Fairy Tale"

"As the desert is one of his habitual homes and dawn an especially uneventful hour, the Jinni is often mindlessly circling under the morning star in the form of a stray bird. From up there it's easy to catch sight of a line of dust kicked up by a column of asses and camels plodding across the sand. He's careful to keep out of sight, the better to follow without causing a commotion. That way, toward dusk when the steward signals for camp to be pitched, he can move in closer among the calm and unsuspecting women; the women who sometimes accompany the tradesmen on their long desert crossings. Sometimes the Jinni likes to get them flapping by upsetting tables set for supper, by blowing out the lamps in a single blast. At other times he enjoys the thick atmosphere of the women's tent and is content to compose his presence in the subtle vapors that tickle their noses, the hemp smoke that makes them sleepy, even to merge with the night music they play on their flutes. But in either case, flapping or serene, he's always the visitor in each of their 3 A.M. dreams, the loving dreams peculiar to that hour.

"What's not so peculiar is this. Loving doesn't mean much unless it's real, another story altogether—that one in a thousand nights out in the desert, silent and still. As usual the Jinni was out there breaking up that calm spell of desert; coming in as a cold gust of wind to swirl the stars around, a crack of lightning to charge the neutral air. And as a matter of course he moved on, drawn by the presence of foreigners, white ones; actually, two of them, lying there side by side in the back of a Jeep. Parked at the edge of the desert just where the sand begins to blow across the road, there was a sleeping man and a restless woman who grew calm the instant the Jinni caught hold of her hand and pulled her gently into the fabric of the night. Ordinarily there's a little struggle, if only for the sake of appearances. But this one was different. She made herself comfortable inside this great cloak of darkness, not at all surprised when he told her, 'Angels are formed of light, men of the dust and earth, I of the subtler substances in between.' When he set her down out there on those wasted stretches, she was not alarmed to witness the permutations of his existence from a lion to a wolf, to a jackal, scorpion, snake. Nor was she particularly impressed when he kicked up a storm; first hail, then rain. By slow, steady degrees the sight of the night unfolding in the bright desert moonlight made her grow calmer and calmer, and it made him wonder—'If only I could prolong the effect. . . . '

"By morning he had acquiesced to his fate.

"Being human she belonged to the level, solid world, and there she would stay. Being of subtler substance he realized there was nothing for him but to belong to her, become part of her, be the breath of life to her. So he came out of the distance as a pillar of sand dancing around her in a wide circle, closing in, lifting her, carrying her back to the Jeep. He heard a distant echo. He was fading to a soft whisper, a wisp of breath passing through her lips . . . lips which for the first time began to move and to speak, capturing his attention and holding him there at the back of her throat. For it seemed that he was back at the beginning, that with the sound of her voice he had arrived at the source of his long, untold existence. It was spellbinding, really—that voice of hers that made words that were him, the Night always unfolding into other nights, beings, entities, shapes that piled up, a dizzying and dumbfounding edifice which spilled over into an intricate system of spaces, a world within a turning world of hours, eons, time fanning out around him, the One-Upright among the horizontals, the Visitor, the Man of Women's Dreams as she called him. She called him in a breathless voice that ran on. "Oh you desert night! One minute you are all and everything and in an instant. I'm here. What can it mean? It's been said that these things happen, that there's chance, lucky stars, meetings at the hour of destiny . . . over and over it's been said until in an instant it rhymes with drop dead. I've had it, I'm done with you in a word. Actually two of them: THE END."

THE VOICE THAT MAKES THE NIGHT—CHARLOTTE SNOW, ACCORDING TO HER FRIEND FRANCINE ROSE

The first time she came over there was rain, one of those soft gentle rains that go deep. "Fine for the country," Charlotte said: but we were having lunch under my skylight where that gentle April rain became a steady drip, drip, drip. The next time it was the sun, a peaked glare I never noticed until we sat there under the skylight unable to breathe without sending up clouds of dust. It was under the pretext of eating that we kept on meeting, circling slowly and fixedly around lunches, dinners, late-night snacks, meals ever later in the night. She liked the night because it was always young. She liked eating in public places where for hours we could sit unnoticed, giggling like girls—girls who had no need for the likes of a boy. As if to demonstrate this, Charlotte would sometimes pencil on a moustache and order a big cigar. She liked only restaurants where cigars could be had, cigars and clean bathrooms, and eventually she liked only one restaurant,

"Lady Astor's." It had a corner booth with velvet curtains which, for a price, the waiter would close—with a smile. She liked this best of all: privacy in public. And in there, a girl I was not. Neither was I a woman. I was all legs and arms, bumping legs and arms always knocking over the wine bottle. I was eyes, they got caught, locked in the longest moment, the moment of recognition. I had a mouth with words flying out of it, words that collided with hers. The collision produced a startling mutation of a language; the deepest of privacies was this. This gave us more than food, than sex, more than a body knows. We were indistinct from our mutated language, our intricate system of intimacy . . . that was who we were. To exist like that we *had* to meet more, more. I made the arrangements, made the "Lady Astor" waiter smile really, really big. And there in our curtained booth we evolved, producing a mutation of the mutation as our dialect gave way to crypto-speech. With initials we encoded vast subjects. Initials, our dots and dashes, also tapped out the lesser topics—the C.G.'s (cute guys; i.e., witless souls trapped in good bodies) and the occasional A double C double S (academic clothing covering some-kind-of-structure; i.e., a not-dumb man). When Charlotte was in between jobs she made a living practicing O.C. (outfit control, or designing clothes for the fashionable set). And when she had to leave town unexpectedly she sent me a telegram: "Everyone in the C. is on I.P. Not my I. of L. Not even C.B.N.C. K's x 10. P.S." Or. "Everyone in the City (New York) is on image patrol (modern narcissism). Not my idea of life. Not even close but no cigar. Lots of kisses. P.S."

(According to Francine, Charlotte always signs her messages *P.S.* to indicate there will be more coming, and in her replies, Francine always underscores her signature with the address below, the site where everything began.)

32 EAST FIRST STREET, NEW YORK CITY

Late in February 1980, Ricky Dent was assigned to keep an eye on Havana Lamotte, a tenant in the basement of the building. Havana was new to New York's Lower East Side but not to intelligence. She would always be under surveillance for the sympathies announced in her name; a rare instance of there possibly being an answer to the worn-out, the usually rhetorical: what's in a name? A questioning type the super at #32 was not. To him "Havana" announced soul-mate, a match made in heaven (a not-so-rare claim filed under another story altogether). The more pertinent file:

> Havana Haydée Lamotte, no known aliases.
> Born 1952, Artemisia, Cuba.
> Father, Ramon, left Cuba with mother, Beatriz, in February 1958. Ramon Lamotte died under mysterious circumstances in April 1958, though a preliminary investigation into his 'drowning' turned up no underworld ties, insurance policies, etc. Conclusion: suicide. Beatriz Lamotte became active in anti-Cuban (communist) activity around the time of her daughter's birth. She has gone on public record—May Day party, Miami, 1970—to the effect that the daughter, Havana, is a legacy of Castro's Cuba (?). For details regarding sexual relations between Beatriz Lamotte and Fidel Castro and any subsequent 'issue'—see M-14, paragraph 73. Mother Beatriz' comment regarding legacy may indicate that the daughter, like herself, was to become active in the NY-Miami mouth network, disseminating propaganda.* Beatriz Lamotte retains same address since her husband's immigration: 3718 Fairlawn Drive, Coconut Grove, Miami, Florida. Havana Lamotte makes irregular but frequent trips between mother's home and New York where she maintains no permanent address.
> *Note: considering Lamotte's family background there is always the very likely chance she is involved in something more.

Always the very likely chance she is involved in something more, something. . . .

It was a long time since contract agent Ricky Dent had been active in the anti-Castro campaign, had approved of such proposals as infusing Castro's shoes with a chemical that would cause his hair to fall out. But once reactivated by the Lamotte assignment, Dent worked double-time, almost instantly closing the gap between Havana Lamotte in the basement and Francine Rose upstairs under her skylight. The logic was assisted by evidence: Lamotte's twenty-four hour courier service and Rose's personal correspondence, a handful of documents written in 'code.' Included were messages received, drafts of replies sent, scraps adrift from the sender-receiver matrix pointing to the likelihood of bigger operations circling out from a clump of papers dropped in the garbage. Another point. Dent found other assistance drifting along those littered Lower East Side streets, streets given to all manner of paper products.

—The 7th Precinct police have reams of records with statistics characterizing the environs as a fourteen by seven block area where there are more murders committed than anywhere else in Manhattan, except in Harlem.

—The N.Y.U. Graduate Library has several Ph.D. theses written by aspiring urban sociologists concerned with the unusual and complex demographic features of a multi-ethnic, multi-racial contiguity and, as gentrification slips into the vocabulary, theses swell, shelves lengthen.

—The quotidian is printed up. In big pictures and a little bit of text the local dailies report the week's obligatory three-alarm fire, drug bust, body in a bag wedged between two abandoned buildings. And the less frequent 'human interest story': Is the richest-country-in-the-world becoming like Calcutta, New Delhi, places where the street is a dormitory, rows of poor bedding down at night?

By daylight the City's homeless appear larger than life, like the TV character, The Hulk, whose body expands to giant proportions, though the humans in question here may have no muscles at all. These giant forms may be tiny people built up from layers of clothing, from wrappings of paper and plastic, muffled up to the chin, the face exposed; the construction then continues. Heads are turbaned or bedecked with countless caps or with just one hat made from brown bag after brown bag fitted one inside another. Embellishing the surface are idiosyncracies of adornment—more buttons than a general, pop-top medals, aluminum foil fringe, magnetic tape streamers, cellophane bows, safety pins, paper-clip garlands, more stuff made in U.S.A. Not French, not on the L.E.S.

A reporter from one of the dailies made such a mistake in identification when attracted to one of the more fashionable homeless. Her idiosyncratic taste—rhinestones and dime store jewels, anything that glitters. Any resemblance to a French woman was genesis made simple, an overeager journalist's splice job—a glittering old woman alive in 1980 on First Avenue/La Môme Bijou-Miss Diamonds, already old in 1932 in a Montmartre night spot.

A little research at the library would have steered the reporter to moments when Ziegfeld Girls appeared regularly in back page tidbits of morning editions of *The Herald*. Having been seen at certain parties, escorted and twirled through after hours life, the Girls made sparks in the daily machinery, some of which didn't just fizzle out. Some big wheels and a smoking gun: a tidbit like that marches from the gossip columns onto the front page.

STANFORD WHITE SHOT DEAD BY MILLIONAIRE HARRY THAW
Playboys in the Garden

The time is 1906; the place, Madison Square Garden; the incident marches around on more recently written pages.

". . . it seems established that White, although a devoted husband and father, was also a determined seducer of young girls.

"In 1901, White met a showgirl called Evelyn Nesbitt, from Ziegfeld's Floradora chorus. She was then sixteen, and looked even younger, but White seduced her. The millionaire Harry Thaw, who was jealous of White on various other grounds, also admired her. Thaw eventually married her, in 1905, suffered greater jealousy, and shot White dead fourteen months later in Madison Square Garden's Restaurant."

Writing in 1976 Martin Green also notes: "Thaw, too, saw himself as a great lover and bravura personality. When he came into his fortune on his twenty-first birthday, he gave a dinner for a hundred actresses, each of whom found a gift of jewelry beside her plate."

A hundred actresses wadded up in three words, seventeen characters of type, a spitball sailing beyond visibility but not out of earshot. Winifred Abel, Irene Arnold, Yvonne Bendkowski, Virginia Blatt, Carlota Bohm, Minnie Briscoe, Adele Brown, Naomi Buchanen, Isabell Capota, Ardell Capra, Rosemary Claire Casey, Dorothea Charles, Lucille Clapper, Estelle Cocco, Ruth

Cory, Josephine Cuomo, Olive Daphnis, Opal Dauber, Pearl Dauber, Wilhemina Dean, Ester DeGarcia, Gladys Vista Dixon, Hattie Doniger, Lili Dorn, Blanche Drakonakis, Pauline Durkin, Sarah Eberhard, Iris Ehrlich, Maxine Emspack, Lydia Evans, Frieda Evers, Catherine Fanning, Edith Fisberg, Lillian Flores, Dora Fortini, Veda Fuchs, Amelia Gelfand, Meredith Glazer, Annabell Green, Stella Guest, Flo Harrison, Jeanette Hart, Dot Herman, Henrietta Hopkins, Crystal Hutchins, Anna Ivany, Cora Jessup, Lili Jones, Angeline Jusino, Faye Kaiser, Mildred Keely, Ruby Kelley, Cecelia King, Joan Louise Koblentz, Phoebe Koppel, Esther Kozic, Louise LaBarbara, Hannah Landau, Edna Lord, Eloise Maxfield, Patricia McBride, Sylvia Miller, Hazel Moran, Ada Mullter, Myra Neff, Allegra Nugent, Margaret Nye, Catherine O'Hagen, Marion Oliver, Eugenia Owings, Evelyn Pesking, Ava Phipps, Ginnie Pomeranz, Bea Purdy, Geraldine Putnam, Virginia Ricks, Christine Rhodes, Nadine Richter, Louisa Robertson, Agnes Ross, Hope Rupenthal, Beatrice Samuels, Dawn Sawyers, Celia Schneider, Ethel Schultz, Cynthia Shatkin, Isabell Snyder, Emmaline Swazey, Madeline . . . the litany like the F-train stops here at the intersection of First Street and First Avenue.

At five o'clock: traffic backed up for minutes on end, blocks and blocks of cars momentarily caught in the First and First nexus. Quadraphonic leakage from car radios tuned to 'Shadow Traffic' sent down from helicopters on the watch for gridlock. On the respective four corners, much of the world is represented here. Abandon the orderly right angles of intersecting streets for "nexus," two crossing diagonals, an X. Jews and Arabs occupy the ends of one axis, and on the other, the more obscure coupling of Eastern Europe and the Mediterranean, a Polish restaurant opposite a quick-stop cafe run by Greeks. Aside from corners tacked down by businessmen, minority groups claim the surrounding area as home, as do individuals living in varying degrees of anonymity and flamboyance, disorderly crowds heading homeward at five o'clock, jaywalking the First-First intersection. X is home base for Madeline Tarkington, or Mad Madeline, as she's known.

She's known for such peculiarities as reeling off alphabetical order seventy-five years after the fact; also for delivering whole punctuated paragraphs when senility shifts from the singed pin-point of a smoking gun, when the fog that comes with age re-cedes to reveal a vista.

The pinpoint. Mothered by a show girl, Madeline is one of un-counted people biologically fathered by Stanford White, left with a dangling genetic blank spot, nothing to flesh it out.

The vista. ". . . All night fruit markets, flower stalls, liquor stores, newsstands, you could get anything you wanted at all hours on Eighth Avenue. We lived around here to be near the theaters and agents, a district full of small studios with one win-dow on an air shaft. Mr. Fishbach, he had 70, 80, 100 of them in his row houses and he didn't bother much with formalities, just pulled out a lease-like paper with a room number at the top fol-lowed by rows of dotted lines. You signed, crossing out the name above. Only women tenants, that was about his only rule, and it had him hauling his 225 pounds of overweight back and forth in front of his buildings, chain smoking Camels, muttering about 'my girls.' We came to him through the grapevine, went away when someone gave up or got a better job or married. Sad good-byes, happy good-byes, and lots of resentment because I couldn't tell which was which, work/marriage, I always said at least there's more to alimony than unemployment checks, good luck. I always bombed with the girls. They didn't like my jokes, didn't like how I wouldn't share my studio, how I never went around after the show with some decent looking guy. Then I got my hair cropped. So. I was a lesbian after all. And who was I to blow the whistle on gossip? At home it gave me some privacy, and on the other hand, the very idea kept the girls from stretch-ing their imaginations far enough to see me going down to the piers. Early in the morning, even with eyes swollen from lack of sleep, there's no mistaking that pretty swaying movement through the haze lifting off the water. See them little behinds coming down the gang plank? Each one, each one alone is even more pretty—a swell of smooth muscle flinching a little at the first kiss of concrete on the sole of a black polished shoe. Oh, sailors. You linger for a minute and they're moving off, bunches of spit-shined toes pointed toward midtown. Thank god for wind. Still two of them trying to light a match, a real pair, Mr.

Mutt and Jeff, though the tall one didn't think so. Didn't think much of my hairdo, either, until it got topped off with his cap. That's how they do it, cap you for a weekend. And the short one? Pascal shook his head slightly and backed off a few steps. Roger was so much taller, he had to lean down to kiss that sad face. When Roger patted him on the bottom, the sad boy fiddled with his buttons, and with Roger's arm around his shoulders, Pascal said nothing all the way to the Village—just more long faces when the coffee finally came.

'You think this American coffee's shit. I'll tell you what's shit. You, if you don't stop whining. What if I leave you on your own? Just you and Louie, eh? Then see how it goes.'

Pascal's going got better after that. All weekend he never peeped about sleeping on the floor of my tiny foyer with his feet in the closet. On the last morning he was still being charming when he climbed into bed. Laying his head on Roger and peeking through those curls of chest hair, he asked very sweetly if I'd come down for a good-bye wave. I agreed, since it was November, cold enough to pin on my new raccoon collar, have my first hot chocolate of the season, even better, some hot buttered rum. A lot of that got drunk the day the *La Sylvette* sailed. In its seven state rooms passengers were probably listening to their friends' I-told-you-so about booking passage on an old freighter. After a three hour delay with engine trouble their champagne was gone, same for the bon-voyage spirit, which was still going strong among the girls who'd come down to see off their sailors. We didn't mind not being allowed on board, not on the corner of Water Street where rounds of rum only cost a dime. In "Smokey's" we didn't mind anything, except for Jeanette. 'My Charlie,' she wailed holding up her glass. 'Oh come on, Jeanette. How can you cry for Charlie when there's a whole boat load of them out there?' And you can bet they weren't looking too pretty down there in the hold, sweat dripping between the cheeks of those hard little behinds, dirty jerseys sticking to their chests. Forget about pretty down there. Valves are being opened, cartons restacked. With luck a guy can duck out of the terrible heat and noise for a quick smoke. Hurrying sailors rib each other with a 'make tracks punk,' 'hey baby dig my hard on,' 'oh beat off.'

And always on the move down those narrow corridors, there's a figure casting a shadow over every inch of the ship. Forget about the captain. Remember the name, Louie Paradise. He had a ticket all right. Dope, that was Louie's ticket; morphine sewed in the lining of his jacket, sold to the lonely, the homesick, anyone dumb enough to get hooked on it. The fun started when the needle happy ran out of money. Halfway across the Atlantic without a sucker to put the touch on, they'd come whining to Louie and he'd meet them in the showers. He liked playing god in there, ordering them down on their hands and knees, sticking it to them in their ass. Maybe no one heard Louie scream the night Pascal took it in the mouth, but if Louie was out of commission for a few days with some teeth marks in his meat, that was nothing compared to the infected track mark running up Pascal's leg. One dirty needle was all it took and the *La Sylvette* came into Marseilles with a stiff in its slow. The captain escorted Louie to the Chief of Police. A halfhour later they were standing on headquarter's steps, buttoning up their pea coats, the Mistral in their ears. When the papers asked for a statement, the Chief said, 'That's what the Marseilles hoodlums do, they kill each other.' Think of it, think of it. . . . ''

The fog is back. The blurry trail is about death on a ship, it's like murder in a hotel, the air never quite clears, little things bring it all back.

Three picture postcards held together with a rubber band

Burnt toast

Dead batteries

Little things are piling up around Madeline as she forages in the garbage for the stuff of her material life ordered according to edible, usable, beautiful. In the reject pile go loose pages, scraps adrift from the sender-receiver matrix.

"Take 'em Sonny. Take 'em if you're that dumb."

And take 'em he did, "Sonny" a.k.a. Ricky Dent. When he waved his evidence under Francine Rose's nose, the smell of garbage was pretty sweet compared to the odorless creep of fanaticism, desperation, and the confusion. Had Dent concluded that coded messages descended to the basement to be disseminated into the world, or was it the other way round—that Lamotte scurried back from her contacts to the woman upstairs, who disguised secrets in the letters of the alphabet? Francine's attempts to make head or tails of it belabored her conversation with friends, whose attention spans had been taxed by efforts to grasp what actually had transpired under drops of rain, among particles of dust, behind velvet curtains; by efforts to puzzle out what third person had provided information about the nexus point linking all that to-ing and and fro-ing of street people, reporters, agents, guns. Ricky Dent packs a .38 automatic, German made perfection popularized in 007 spin offs. But weary of details, friends grew impatient with the Dent affair, began to ask questions or talk among themselves.

"Was it likely that so complicated a plot would all depend on the unwitting cooperation of one mercurial young woman about to leave for England?"

or

"Francine Rose. An obsessive personality! Always making a federal case out of her own personal problems."

No one said: that what one really is, is knowing oneself as a product of a historical process to date which has deposited in you an infinity of traces without leaving an inventory; the job of producing an inventory is the first necessity. Or, that many people find their way to the general through the personal, the individual. These were quotations underlined in books Charlotte Snow was reading in a bed-sit in Islington, a borough of North London where she'd taken up residence. She'd described the situation in a letter to Francine. "I'm becoming a repository, a compendium of statements that're being committed to memory. Someday I'll be like a vast, indexed reference book that can flip to its own pages at will. Naturally there's a trick, a system. I'm using one described in *The Art of Memory* by Frances A. Yates, a medieval system . . . too intricate to go into here. But essentially you image a building constructed of rooms and each designated room is a subject heading where particular material's stored. So the material's not just conserved; it can also be located in a flash. Among other things one has to keep the imaged structure from becoming some dizzying and dumbfounding edifice that will topple over. That means starting with a sound foundation.

Sound looney? So is living in an Islington building crawling with armchair radicals tossing off buzz words and received ideas, pearls before the American swine, me, who's wandering down the hallways of medieval metaphysics. Still, the system seems to be working. My imaged building is a standard middle-class house, and when I got your letter about upstairs, down-stairs Dent, I wandered into the Closet and flipped directly to *Conspiracy*, A. Summers: 'The American intelligence community is so sprawling a creation that it spawns compartments where not even those in charge can be sure what is going on. One such was its anti-Castro division, consisting in 1962 of 600 Americans, most of them case officers, plus upward of 3,000 contract agents in and out of Cuba. The Americans no less than the exiles were committed to their cause. There was the proposal, for example, to infuse Castro's shoes with a chemical compound that would cause his hair to fall out. (Once bald and unbearded, his charis-matic charm would disappear.) Also a specially treated cigar to make him incoherent during one of his speech making mara-thons. Or spraying LSD in his broadcasting studio for much the same effect.' Actually, Francine, when you first sent word of the Dent business I just rolled my eyes and stuck there on the back of my eyelids was the old question we always used to ask: I.T.I.L.O.E.? If your alpha-speak is a little rusty, I'll spell that out when you get here. I *am dying* to see you again. Please try to bring some news of Edgar Krebs and some all cotton sweatshirts. Much love, P.S."

27 March 1980

Dear Charlotte,

Did you get the message I called? Whoever answers your phone isn't terribly cooperative. I had as much trouble getting across to them as I've been having with calls to West Bengal, a subtle introduction to my change of plans. I plan to see you still in London but on the return trip in June. By then will your head be swollen beyond recognition, the size of that house you're stuffing with 'material'? Or will you have invented something like the flying buttress to hold up your densely packed cranium?

Technologists are trying to invent computers that can think. So what's the idea of trying for the reverse, housing a storage and retrieval system, becoming a human computer that doesn't think? Such are my infantile terrors. I've always had a near phobia about mind control, waking up in *1984* with a Roman Polanski script: "This isn't a dream, this is really happening!" I want to say *the future is now* without being glib, I want shiny coin phrases. Not slogans stamped on buttons and T-shirts like hip brand names strangers use to find each other. Not frozen phrases like flash cards that teach you to recognize word groups in 1/32 of a second, no meaning, let alone spelling. I.T.I.L.O.E.? Not that either. Alpha-speak is everywhere from DDT to FMLN-FDR, both inescapable, poison and politics. But when we see each other again let's work on the lost art of plain English, inefficient as it may be in a world of initials. The FMLN-FDR is a coalition of the Revolutionary Democratic Front (FDR) and the five guerilla groups in the Farabundo Martí National Liberation Front (FMLN). These five groups are the Salvadoran Communist Party (PLS), the Popular Forces of Liberation (FPL), the Revolutionary Army of Central American Workers (PRTC), the People's Revolutionary Army (ERP), and the Armed Forces of National Resistance (FARN). Within each of these groups, there are further factions and sometimes even further initials, as in the PRS and LP-28 of the ERP. That's public information.

And Havana Lamotte has an equally complicated life story bound up in split factions which as *you* say is too intricate to go into here, will have to wait till I meet you in the falling rain, June in London on the P.E.—plain English not Hampstead—Heath.

In the meantime I'm getting to know Havana. She's staying in the spare room. (Among other things we agree that under the circumstances it's a little too symbolic to be living below ground in the basement.) Up here it's Insomniacs Anonymous. She tells me her nightmares, I tell her mine.

. . . A woman wearing a red veil comes walking up the driveway from the far end where she's just stepped out of a shiny black car. She has some trouble negotiating the icy patches and the wind keeps blowing her coat straight out. Then suddenly the wind dies and her key is turning in the front door lock, her footsteps are on the stairs, even the silver charms of her bracelet are jingling, jingling in the quiet of that long windless moment. . . .

What does it mean? We don't need a shrink for this one. Havana is haunted by an image of a three-piece suit packing a .38 Walther PPK and commiserating with M.M. which doesn't stand for Marilyn Monroe. Havana happened to see poor old Mad Madeline going through the garbage on the afternoon Dent came snooping around in his flannels. So one part of the puzzle's no longer a mystery. The papers I'd thrown out got recycled through Madeline and, need I say, Dent never had to dirty his hands.

Enclosed is the part that haunts me. As you know this recent event isn't the first time Madeline has intervened in our lives, and it's in your words that I register a little detonation, the sickening eruption of a déjà vu. Maybe there's a corner in your memory system for the enclosed article you wrote so long ago for, god help us, the *House Organ*.

I'm writing at such length, sorry. I'll try to be brief.

All cotton sweatshirts are in the mail. Black and blue and white.

As for Edgar Krebs, he left for an early vacation without a word and our temporary super is Rudolf Brenner from next door who now goes by the name Rainer Berlin, rechristened for his favorite poet and the city of his birth. What he knows about Rilke and Berlin would fill a space the size of the tiny heart tattooed on his shoulder which carries a burden no heavier than the weight of some chains looped through the epaulets of his leather jacket—just another character jingling along, a guy in his own movie complete with sound effects. Oddly enough, he's scouting locations for an 'actual' film he's involved with as the art director; some cops and robbers remake starring local leather-and-steel talent. He thinks my apartment is perfect for it, all those points of view(!). Shots down through the skylight, up through the hole in the floor, tracking through the sliding door to next door . . . dumm da dum dum. If it'll pay the rent while I'm gone, I'm game. Rainer is still Rudolf, still asks after you. "Well, well Rose Red how is Snow White?" I didn't tell him not all women are attracted to fairy tales with One-Uprights stalking around. In-

stead of double negatives I searched for the tape of your radio program and when I couldn't find it, I gave him the typescript to read. Is that OK? The more I send out of here the more nice and empty it becomes. Insomnia has me on the night shift. At this hour my assistants, strategically positioned around the apartment, are working tirelessly to keep the place reasonably together. A Roach Motel in the corner is collecting bugs on some surface, sweet and sticky. Under the stove, a package of D-Con poison is inviting mice to their last supper at my expense. A small fortune passes hands for these and other contraptions such as a penguin shaped one on the tap filtering heavy metals out of the water, a pyramid shaped ionizer revitalizing polluted air. I pay for contraptions sold by the same companies that produce the problems that destroy the house we all live in. Is this why I've a reputation for making mountains out of molehills? Mountains. When I go to them periodically for some fresh air and for some kind of mental space that only comes with practice . . . never mind. Some people jog, some sit very very still. It'll be more than nice to see you on my way back. Somedays I miss your company to the point of distraction. I think this was one of them. Much love,
Francine
#32 E.F.S.

32, 34 EAST FIRST STREET, NEW YORK CITY

A typical screw-up. This morning when I came downstairs all the mail for #32 had been delivered here by mistake. People I don't know read *Newsweek* and *Soviet Life,* get thin blue aerograms from Dublin, bills from a West Side doctor, from a collection agency in Omaha. A typical screw-up and too suddenly, there's a chink in the venetian blinds of people I don't know.

#32, 34 are identical twins from the pink and black tiled entrances to the matching skylights giving access to the adjoining roofs. There's a huge telescope up there when the weather permits. When nights are clear our super searches for comets, the one he'll sight before any other amateur astronomer's known as

113

a streak across the sky. If Halley did it so can Edgar Krebs, he's fond of saying. He's fond of the ring of "Kreb's Comet," plans a traveling laser light show bearing that title, part of the someday when he leaves the roof and is an itinerant astronomer with his scheme packed up in a couple of aluminum suitcases.

"Earth to Egbert, earth to Egbert." I hear kids yelling in the hall when they're not pumping quarters into Donkey Kong video games Edgar could probably program in his sleep. I hear footsteps overhead and rap three times on the skylight. Silence means call the cops. Two raps means it's Edgar conducting his roof top vigil. I go up for a look. His sight is trained on his favorite target. "The fashionable world, a tremendous orb nearly five miles around, is in full swing, and the solar system works respectfully at its appointed distances."

Me: "A little respectful backing off seems perfectly in order here since it's physical space not knowledge everyone's after. Let's call for a moratorium on greed. Hands off the sky, everyone zip up their pants and pipe down."

He: "Oh, come on. The search for extraterrestrial life is, in the opinion of many, the most exciting, challenging, and profound issue not only of this century but of the whole naturalistic movement that has characterized the history of Western thought for 300 years. What is at stake is the chance to gain a new perspective on man's place in nature."

Me: "Let's begin the search with fingering the question, is there intelligent life on earth? Is there a naturalist for attending to minute phenomena, for reading between the lines?"

He: "Don't go metaphorical on me. Facts. I want some plain old ordinary facts. This isn't Egypt, we're not talking in riddles."

Me: "What is this civilization in which we find ourselves? What are the ceremonies and why should we take part in them? What are these professions and why should we make money out of them? Where in short is it leading, the processions of the sons of educated men?"

He: "Well, Alfred North Whitehead and Bertrand Russell had a fruitful collaboration, *Principia Mathematica*. Their work on "logistic language" had been preceded by efforts to produce an international language which would bring the world closer together. The first to be widely used was Volapük, invented in 1880 by an Austrian priest. This was followed seven years later by Esperanto, but the mathematician Peano felt these had failed to escape from the arbitrary and illogical syntax of tongues that had evolved in the chance manner of nature. In 1903 he produced Interlingua, derived from classical Latin but with a simplified syntax. It is still widely used in abstracting scientific articles."

> (My ignored interruption: "Probably he has got no red blood in his body. Somebody put a drop under a magnifying glass and it was all semicolons and parenthesis. Oh, he dreams of footnotes, and they run away with all his brains. They say when he was a little boy, he made an abstract of 'Hop o' My Thumb' and he's been making abstracts ever since. Ugh!")

"These developments have lead Hans Freudenthal, Professor of Mathematics at the University of Utrecht, to attempt extending the "logistic language" of Whitehead and Russell into something intelligible to beings with whom we have nothing in common except intelligence. He calls it "Lincos" as a short form of "Lingua Cosmica." The logical exposition of the language as might take place in an extended interstellar message is contained in his book, *Lincos: Design of a Language for Cosmic Intercourse.* Actually, he pointed out, such a language already may be established as the vehicle for cosmic intercourse."

Me: "Great. Everyone speaking the same tongue, singing the same anthem. Fuck cosmic intercourse, celestial syntax."

"Oh, come on."

"You come on!"

"I don't believe you, I really don't."

"No one asked you to." Someone, however is coughing in the shadows. "Oh, it's Francine, hi."

As witnesses to Edgar's near nightly vigil, Francine and I became familiar with all his schemes and with the practical side of his talents, which run to anything electrical, mechanical, even structural. He's helped us to make our apartments burglar-proof, our cranky radiators give off steam, and when we decided to make our lives simpler, he had us chipping through the correct spot in the common wall of our apartments. If Gulf & Western could do it so could we. That was our scheme, Francine and mine. If considered in the light of multinationals, our merger, a consortium of two, will not a big deal make. Neither will darkness make do, nor a gray zone where someone, however, *is* always coughing in the shadows, infecting the entire organism out to the extremities, our leaping-off site. No big deal, except for the laws of nature, which state that no two bodies can occupy the same space at the same time. Ricky Dent, his boss, would like to be a law that certain; know which bodies occupy what space when. They don't like, maybe no one likes strategem, deception, facts giving way to a sprawling fiction, the lives we live:

Two people become one on paper by drawing up a contract and pooling their resources to exist as a stronger economic unit, an imagined third person. Conversely, one person exists as many, a string of aliases and a.k.a.'s, when there really is something to the what's-in-a-name homily. When originally Francine and I drew up our contract we provided for inevitable complications. For example, when Francine went away she replaced herself in the unit. Now Havana Lamotte upholds a share in domestic economics my salary cannot withstand alone.

I work in the Lincoln Center Library, Theater Division, where lives of performers are bequeathed to eternity. We disassemble their scrapbooks, photographs, reviews, love letters; we cut and paste. We, some of us, work late after our bosses go home. The place then is ours, a treasure house of free stationery this fluorescent lit sanctuary where the free Xerox machine is humming away. I copy things for Francine.

A typescript: *TWICE-TOLD TALES, an Ecological Test made from Recycled Material;* adapted by Charlotte Snow; footnotes by Richard Burton; additional annotation by Gustave Flaubert.

An article: *AT NIGHT. The Biography of an Object* by Charlotte Snow. The object of this study is a piece of jewelry, or at least it was once all of a piece, a necklace of Egyptian origin associated with Hathor. Legend recounts that at the origin of time, men conspired against their Creator, Re. After considering the matter, Re decided to send his Eye (consciousness) in the form of a lioness to chastise the insurgents. She was called Sekhmet, meaning "powerful," an aspect of Hathor. Sekhmet wrought havoc and would have devoured all humanity had not Re, stricken with regret, then had the ground covered with red-dyed beer in place of blood, so that Sekhmet, deceived by the color, drank up the liquid, became drunk and fell asleep, thus sparing mankind. This took place, however, very far to the south of Egypt. It fell to Thoth, lord of writing and time, to bring Sekhmet back into Egypt. Barely had the two arrived in Aswan when Thoth plunged her into the waters of Abaton in order to "quench her heat." And thus it was that the blood-thirsty lioness was transformed into the gentle cat, Basket, one of the aspects of Hathor.

But not all is a lioness brought under control and made to pussyfoot through all eternity.

Under the multiple names that evoke her countless aspects, Hathor represents a synthesis of Egyptian notions concerning cosmogenesis, and as such she is of a different dimension than Aphrodite, with whom the Greeks mistakenly identified her. For despite her female epithets, including "Mistress of Love," she isn't the Feminine Principle. Under the name of Neith, for example, she is addressed as "Lady of Sais," meaning two-thirds masculine and one-third feminine.

I read the first page of the article while the Xerox machine hummed away copying things Francine needed in preparation for her departure. She's gone to mountains so high and remote not even the tools of surveillance travel that far. Even if it sounds like escaping she lives with wanderlust contracted at an early age and reports this as fact. "There are places where there is no television, yet: Darjeeling, which is perching at a high altitude and for days nothing, white nothing, from the Windemere's windows, the renowned hotel in the clouds. When a hard wind blows, Mt. Everest is standing there and . . . Darjeeling is perching in the foothills of the Himalayas. In these lowly heights soft are the sounds brought here on a strange, fitting breeze, dizzying tease, oh jeez, please stop. And indeed one does become accustomed to always having an airflow in the head, to the unremitting rustle of silk prayer flags, of deep moaning prayers circling up from the valley. Monks down there have a hard-to-grasp notion of words as living things. Thus anything committed to writing cannot be destroyed unless the life of it is passed on in a ceremonial fire; colored smoke warming the atmosphere with

117

the breath of life. At a far distance from the monastery, the Windemere is a relic of the British Raj still serving high tea on a landscaped terrace. A piece of paper caught in a bush makes a flap. I release it, a page from *Romeo and Juliet,* the part about love traveling from hand to hand, lip to lip. It makes me laugh, it always has, those two kids all bent out of shape and there's no one here to iron them into the fabric of Darjeeling life. Local residents await the arrival of television, one set which they'll watch in the movie house. I've come to a place where words are living things and where my Darjeeling friends await exotic reflections of faraway places with strange sounding names. They look forward to seeing me on television after a safe journey home which as you know will be soon enough, after London in the falling rain. Love, Francine."

Francine's letters come to Havana and me at the 32-34 complex on East First Street addressed to Carol Riding, the so-called person who simplifies things, clears difficult economic hurdles. And yet, Carol, she comes into existence like neighbors glimpsed in a stack of strange envelopes; these I'm entitled to open, envelopes enclosing an unsolicited credit card from a second rate rent-a-car company, catalogs promoting discounted make-up with a free sample, a request for a signature on a letter protesting the incarceration of Polish intellectuals; but no health insurance policy. No, instead of the one awaited document which would verify our conscious efforts, there comes only Hulkish unarrested expansion into a creature putting on lipstick in the rearview mirror of a rented car with license plates made by convicts as opposed to incarcerated intellectuals. That's not right. A woman is putting on her make-up before picking up a rented car, and on the way she drops a letter of protest in a mailbox. This woman has incessant conversations with Shepherd, a fanciful constant companion, a man I knew briefly in real life in days when the scheme, Francine and mine's, was young. Older is a dry clot of days punctured by dots, dashes, blank spots where caprice whispers and moans. It started on Wednesday. An invisible hand relieved Havana of her pocketbook in a crowded coffee shop. Last night she received an anonymous call from a man in a phone booth at 125th Street and Amsterdam Avenue who claimed he'd found her wallet and other valuables, she could come up and get them, he'd be waiting in front of Harlem Hospital. By morning it's still uncertain if the phone caller, who now calls himself Pinkie, will keep the second rendezvous; if his absence at the first was a true misunderstanding; if this isn't a classic set-up in which the original thief receives a reward for returning stolen possessions as his partners burglarize the victim's apartment known to be vacant while she traipses uptown; if we aren't reasonably justified in assuming an absence of rectitude— "Of what?" Havana snaps, nerves running wild. It started as a joke. Where once I kidded about us assembling in Carol Riding a Frankenstein creature who would probably turn on its makers, Francine was ever serious, reacting with a learned diatribe about *Reason, Rectitude, Justice;* three celestial Graces who appeared before a worrying woman in 1405 "to restore her senses, to explain to her the causes of antifeminism and to reveal womanhood's true nature, and at the same time, they will help her build a fortified city, an ideal city in which all noble women of the past, present, and future can live undisturbed." When it seemed appropriate to the occasion of her leaving, of Havana Lamotte entering, Francine amended her diatribe, said the source of her celestial reference, her friend Charlotte Snow, had strayed too far afield with medievalisms, things eerily Euclidean; at any rate *we* could stick to the principle of the thing. We could, for example, continue along the lines of three Graces in reaction to which Havana had said it was about time we discussed down to earth things, in particular that now anxiously awaited health insurance policy. But it doesn't come; only unsolicited envelopes, unwanted incidents, glimpses and snaps. If we are reasonably justified in assuming an absence of moral integrity, the dictionary's words for "rectitude," the dictionary isn't giving many pointers about how to proceed with a guy named Pinkie who may or may not be waiting in front of Harlem Hospital at noon, three-thirty, five-thirty, he can't make up his mind, his upper hand that jerks us around; us and our masked man, our day's dose of button, button, who's got the button? And so it goes. Hours of relay phone calls to and from Havana, many particulars, reassessments of "personal business" conducted on library time

under the watchful eyes of Miss Millicent Gibbs, the supervisor
. . . after hours of this, I've a mind contracted to a sore spot; only
the tight little curlicue of a snatched purse located in a throbbing muscle in my neck. I am not discussing it with Shepherd,
with whom all conversation is on a nontedious plane, is involun-
tary murmuring—high nonsense on the way home at rush hour.
I am not the only one thus engaged, betrothed to a phantom.
Thousands rushing home and this woman, that man, many are of
the murmuring lips. Many are mouthing their capricious man-
tras, whispers and moans, though rarely in the body to body tight
quarters of the subway where I am a less than anonymous work-
er, thanks to the colors of midnight: black shot with deepest of
blue, a hand-me-down dress inscribed with love of night from
Charlotte to Francine to me spit out of the train, hurrying,
jaywalking.

Upstairs. I wind back the tin top of my kippers in front of the 7
O'Clock News. I hear kids yelling in the hall, footsteps overhead, three and two raps on a pane of glass, and on the roof, a dry
peck for right cheek, left cheek. Edgar's back from vacation, returned to his near nightly vigil and up here all's very still. It's our
tacit agreement to replace scenes unworthy of repetition, it's our
truce to realign a badly tallied invoice, all that he-ing and me-
ing of:

—Ill trained ideologues banging their solitary gongs

—Unmagic mediums through which there passed two separate processions of ghosts

—Faulty instruments streaking the sky on a trajectory heading
for the drink

Many minuses
One plus—all's very still. It's a startling silence, it's the
breathtaking quiet when a long monotonous sound suddenly
breaks off.

NOTES

P.137 Martin Green, *Children of the Sun*, 1976, Basic Books.

P.144 Joan Didion, "In El Salvador," *New York Review of Books,* November 1982.

P. 147 The "ghosts" passing through unmagic mediums. He: Charles Dickens *(Bleak House),* Space Science Board of the National Academy of Sciences, Walter Sullivan *(We Are Not Alone).* Me: Adrienne Rich *(On Lies Secrets and Silence),* Virginia Woolf *(Three Guineas),* George Eliot *(Middlemarch).*

PP. 149-150 Lucy Lamy, *Egyptian Mysteries,* 1981, Thames and Hudson.

P. 152 Christine de Pizan, *The Book of The City of Ladies,* (orig. 1405) 1982, Persea Books

Acknowledgements—editors Ingrid Sischy (*Art Forum*) and Betsy Sussler (*Bomb*) for their previous publication of segments included in the present text.

URSULE
MOLINARO

TOP STORIES #16 $2.50

Sweet Cheat of Freedom
by Ursule Molinaro

2-in-1

TOP STORIES #16 $2.50

Analects of Self-Contempt
by Ursule Molinaro

2-in-1

SWEET CHEAT OF FREEDOM

SWEET CHEAT OF FREEDOM

for John Evans

He had *not* said: No man is truly free, until he has a slave.

No Roman feels free, unless he has a slave: was what he had said. Rather imprudently, perhaps. To the only daughter of his former master, the senator. When the senator had still been his master. Officially as well as *de facto*. Whose only daughter he had tutored for 11½ of her 16   almost 16½   years.

Had begun to tutor nearly 12 summers ago. After the senator became senator, after the death of his senator-father-in-law. When the new senator had decided   with his newly inherited rank   that he wanted his only daughter to grow up to think like a man. And had acquired a Greek thinking-slave, from Sparta, to tutor her to grow up to think like a man. Like the son & heir-to-the-senate he'd been prevented from having, by whatever it was that he had given to his wife. Who was of better Roman birth than he was. Brought home to Rome. From one of the campaigns in southern Gaul & passed on to his better-born wife, before he became senator after the death of his senator-father-in-law. Before he & his better-born wife began to age.

Before he began to resent his equally   though differently

aging wife. A little more each day. For not aging the way he was aging: rather resentfully; obesely. For cheating on nature. By looking younger   & younger than the one year that she was younger than he was.

Because of whatever it was that he had passed on to her, perhaps, that was perhaps delaying the natural aging process of her 39-   almost 39½-year-old   better-born body after preventing it from bearing him other children. Cheating him out of a son, after bearing the only daughter.

Who had grown up to resent her mother.

Whose barely perceptible   rather serene   aging the senator's 45-year-old Spartan-Greek thinking-slave liked to attribute to thinking. Which had perhaps been prompted in the mother's mind by whatever it was that she might have heard him say during much of 11½ years of daily dialogue attempts in which he had tried to involve the only daughter.

Who had perhaps resented her mother's almost daily presence, during much of the 11½ years. From the first day on, perhaps. Walling herself in willful stony deafness against whatever it was that he might be saying.

About a little girl, for instance, who chose boredom in the belief that she was choosing freedom.

Who was probably too little to understand that the only true freedom was freedom of thought. Which many grownups didn't understand either. Ever. For which one had first to learn how to think. Not necessarily like a man. Or like a Roman. But like a human being. The only true hierarchy being a hierarchy of minds . . .

Some of which were better born than others. Not socially better born, necessarily. Although a comfortable social position   of senator parents could be helpful, in certain cases. Wasn't always helpful, however. Induced smugness &/ or laziness, & subsequent boredom in certain cases.

Some of which arrived in the world better-equipped than others. With a head-start, so to speak. Which made it easier for them to reassemble   in detail   the knowledge which the gods took away from man in exchange for his first breath.

Man's first breath blew his mind, so to speak. Wiped his memory-slate clean of most of the subconscious total knowledge of life which man shared with the gods up to the moment of his birth.

Continued to share with the gods in his dreams, after his birth.

When his taking shape, his taking on a specific   the human
     form restricted his grasp of life as a totality to the human experience of life. To his own personal perception.

Which was his tool.

Which he had to use consciously, every day of his life, in order to understand his relationship to the other specific forms of life around him: other men/   animals/   plants/   moun-tains/   rivers/   the sky/   the earth.

To understand all of life by means of his own specific life, as he grew. Up. & older. Toward reabsorption by death. When the gods judged by the sum total of his understanding whether he had succeeded or failed.

Which failed to scale the willful deafness walls of the 4½-5-5½-6-etc.-year-old mind.

Which he continued to try to scale, unsuccessfully, for 11½ years.

Stealthily ignoring 7 to 8 years of boredom-born tantrums.

The subsequent recounting of which   by the mother amused the senator.

Until the tantrums gave way to an equally boredom-born, equally deaf passion for verbal disagreement.

Holding over 3,000 monologues. While: the only daughter nudged her listening mother. Tugged at her listening mother. Poked her listening mother. Climbed one of his legs. Kneaded his lap with her toes. Stared into his eyes. Blew into his ears. His talking mouth. Searched between his thighs with outrageous 4½-5-5½-6-6½-year-old directness.

Which he   & the listening mother   tried not to see. To pay no attention to. On the principle that: what you don't feed cannot live.

On which principle, its positive & its negative applications:

Feeding an affection with attention; a mind with thoughts; a plant with water.

Starving a resentment/ a jealousy by withdrawing your thoughts from the subject   or object; an illness/ a tantrum by ignoring it . . .

he continued to talk. While the mother continued to listen. Both conscientiously paying no attention to the only daughter.

Who disrobed, & marched out of earshot. Past the patio confines of blue-clustering grapes. Into the late-summer muck of the duck pond.

In which she proceeded to roll her 5-year-old nudity until she was pulled out & returned muck-crusted & flailing to the patio. By a weeping girl, a recent slave from southern Gaul, who was anticipating another beating, this one official, administered by the mistress of the house, after an initial unofficial one, administered by painful bruising 5-year old fists.

Which the mistress of the house had ceased to administer   to any of her slaves   after listening to one of his early monologues about the non-violence of true authority.

Which the mistress of the house should perhaps have administered to the muck-crusted 5-year-old bottom of the only daughter, in spite of what she had listened to him say about nonviolence.

About the unruffle-able serenity of a "true" master. Early that summer. During an aromatic morning in a rowboat on the senator's green-mirroring turtle lake. That had lain in seemingly unruffle-able serenity. Dark-brown turtles dropping from the bullrushes like giant bedbugs; ducks & cranes flying crookedly into the air at the almost soundless approach of the rowboat.

Until the vehemence of 4½-year-old boredom finally succeeded in overturning the rowboat in which it had felt held captive.

The subsequent recounting of which amused the senator to the point of laughter.   Which was one of man's —dubious— distinctions from —other— animals. A distinction the senator thought he shared with the gods. Although he had very nearly lost:

1 (& only) 4½-year-old daughter
1 27½-year-old better-born wife
1 18-year-old well-muscled Teuton rowing-slave
& 1 33-year-old Spartan-Greek thinking-slave in the process.

Whose fault it would have been if all 4 of them had drowned. For thinking inadequately.

For not knowing how to capture a 4½-year-old attention. From the first day, the first word, on. For capturing   & holding the mother's 27½-year-old attention instead.

For not quite daring to take physically punitive measures. Which were not only not in keeping with his nonviolence principles, but also contrary to certain basic considerations of prudence: A slave striking his master's 4½-5-5½-6-6½-etc.-etc.-year-old only daughter. In the presence of the 27½-28-etc.-etc.-year-old mother, who had listened to years of his monologues about the laziness of violence. While he   & the mother   continued to ignore the growing only daughter's daily growing boredom.

Preferring to praise the excellence of melon marmalade, when the 6½-year-old flayed an entire field of richly ripe melons which they were passing with a frenzied stick.

When he   & the mother   continued walking. While he continued to talk.

About: "miniature suns, shining from a deep-green foliage-sky."

& about: "the recurrence of the egg shape everywhere in nature. The neuter, still neutral, shape of the fruit/the seed. With its promise of male & female. Before the split into male & female. Into pistil & petals   One split in two, & started talking . . . "

& about: "the all-pervading elementary trinity of earth/ water/ air/ recurring in flesh/ blood/ breath; stem/ sap/ green . . . " Etc. Etc. Etc. Etc. Etc. Etc. Etc. Etc. . . .

Rather than use the frenzied stick on the melon-shaped already blatantly female   6½-year-old bottom.

A subsequent recounting of which   by the sore-bottomed only daughter   might not have amused the senator to the point of gods-shared laughter.

Might, on the contrary, have prompted the not-amused senator to revise his Greek thinking-slave's Spartan tutoring methods by cutting off the slavish hand that had dared strike his master's only daughter. Or, more simply, to cut off the slavish head, to put a stop to the kind of thinking that led to slaves striking their master's only daughter.

Whose increasingly violent boredom-tantrums were well in keeping with Roman patrician tradition: according to the senator's Spartan-Greek thinking-slaves' unrevised thinking.

The same frantic attempts to silence   with screams of childish rage; & later with the screams of victims: of animals, of slaves   the inner voice that was telling them how unfree they were.

Were free perhaps not to listen to their fathers' thinking-slaves, but not free not to listen to the whisper voice inside themselves that kept telling them that they, the proud patricians, the empire builders, the history-makers, were abject menial slaves. To their needs & greeds. To their craving for effect-producing. For constant world-wide attention.

Were more enslaved than the slaves who served them. Who ruled them, by serving them.   Might eventually   some day   start ruling them without continuing to serve them, if the masters continued to ignore their inner whisper voice. Until they'd become unable to ignore the whisper voices of their slaves.

Who were beginning to doubt the self-mastery of their masters. In the different idioms of their different ethnic & social backgrounds. Which their enslaved condition was melting into one language, spoken & understood by all. The language of passive resistance. In echo-response to the suffering inflicted upon most of them by obesely bored masters. Who called their thoughtless   or, on the contrary, their minutely thought-out cruelties: necessary punitive measures. Healthy discipline. When they themselves lacked even the discipline not to overeat. & dieted by proxy, by starving their slaves . . .

Who had somehow begun to hear what the senator's Spartan-Greek thinking-slave had been thinking out loud for 7 to 8 years. In the course of his   less & less prudent; more & more outspoken   daily monologues.

Which they'd begun to repeat to one another. In the different idioms of their different ethnic & social backgrounds.

Which ceased being monologues, after the suddenly listening 12½-year-old only daughter began to contradict whatever she thought she had heard.

Vehemently.

& to repeat to the senator whatever she thought she had heard that she had contradicted.

Incorrectly.

Not understanding whatever it was that he might have said.

Somewhat more prudently, lately.   About: the importance of understanding, for instance, the relative unimportance, the luxury, of being understood . . .

About   with all due respects   Juvenal's somewhat unfortunate saying that: *mens sana in corpore sano* was the greatest gift of the gods.

Treating mind & body as two separate entities. As though the mind were not part of the body. As much as part of body as the hands, the feet. When we needed our whole body to think with. Could understand a concept only after we'd felt its applications with our body.

Which was perhaps why Juvenal was so often misunderstood. Hygienically misunderstood, so to speak. Misquoted, as though he had meant to say that a healthy body was the *conditio sine qua non* of a healthy mind.

Which made about as much sense as saying that a broken leg prevented a man from seeing.

Although it might conceivably prevent him from seeing things in places where his broken leg prevented him from going.

Which made the now-14-year-old now-listening only daughter laugh.

Before   or perhaps after   it occurred to her to burn the soles of one of her father's slave girls' feet with hot stones which she'd ordered the girl to heat. In order to understand the concept of pain.

Which made the senator share in the laughter of his only daughter which both shared with the gods   after she described to him what she had done after what the thinking-slave had said.

Which the now-listening only daughter had perhaps willfully misunderstood.

Was perhaps, making a game of misunderstanding.

A game in which the senator was perhaps sharing, when he repeated to all of Rome what his Spartan-Greek thinking-slave had *not* said.

For every potentially rebellious slave to hear. & to repeat.

To believe that he had actually said: No man is truly free, until he has a slave   After he'd been given his freedom. & a slave of his own.

Whom to set free he was not free enough.

Nor was he free enough to leave Rome & return to Sparta.

Was free enough only to continue living in the small crude house on his former master's grounds in which he had lived for nearly 12 years. Which felt smaller now that he had to share it with his slave. A not-too-bright, not-too-clean girl from southern Gaul whom enslavement had aged prematurely. Sullenly.

Who sullenly practiced   on him   the passive resistance he had preached.

Who felt further degraded by serving a former slave. A former "equal." Whom she mistrusted, because she'd been told what he had not said, after he'd been given his freedom. Which he had no way of rectifying, since the girl spoke neither Greek nor the language of Rome.

Hardly spoke   or washed   at all. A sullen slightly smelly presence. That he felt the unexpected temptation to beat, at times, when she kept persistently in his way, in the smaller-seeming crude house.

Which he no longer had any reason or excuse to leave. Since the senator had deemed that his only daughter was well able to think like a man, like a true Roman, at 16; almost 16½. & that his 45-year-old Spartan-Greek former thinking-slave had therefore no further need to think. Out loud. In the listening almost daily presence of the 39½-year-old mother who continued to age barely perceptibly. Serenely.

Who had sent the Spartan-Greek former-thinking-slave the jug of wine he had just finished drinking. The dregs of which had the color & texture of slowly drying blood.

DONNA **WYSZOMIERSKI**

TOP STORIES #18 $2.50

FORGET ABOUT
YOUR FATHER

& other stories

DONNA WYSZOMIERSKI

FORGET ABOUT YOUR FATHER
& OTHER STORIES

FORGET ABOUT YOUR FATHER

Forget about your father, I told my son. He left me without a dime to chase some young floozy. The kid kept talking about him, it just about broke my heart. Why would you want to be like him, I asked. He admitted it was the guy's height, said it must be my fault he's short. I can't do anything about my genes, I said, you could always get elevated shoes. I took him to a store where the clerk was a friend from way back. He had trouble walking at first, but I had to admit it improved his appearance. I was just starting to relax when the old man shows up and tells the kid he looks ridiculous. You ought to be boosting his ego, I said, why don't you buy him some clothes? All kinds of stuff started coming in the mail, I was embarrassed when the boy wore it. He got these in a thrift shop, I said. We almost came to blows before the kid quieted down.

The next day he announced he wanted to take a modeling course. I was sorry when I heard how much it cost. He came home with a blonde about twenty-eight, the grooming advisor, he called her. I dragged him into the kitchen. She's a little old for you, I said. He asked her to stay for supper. While we were eating she kept looking at my hair. Something on your mind, I asked. Your look's kind of outdated, she said, I could give you a permanent. I wondered if she really thought it would help. We can do wonders these days, she told me. Why don't you come down to the school tomorrow? After she left I asked my son if I'd be intruding. He said not really, she was reasonable.

We got to talking while she rolled up my hair. You know, she told me, your son's very attractive. I want him to go to college, I said, but he wants to be a musician. She said her husband was in a band and they split up over it. Every night he was either playing or practicing, and socially she was on her own. I wouldn't complain, I told her, you have a nice business here. Why would a girl like you want to get married? She said she wanted to have kids some day. Fine, I told her, don't rob the cradle.

They were out late every night. How's the advising coming, I asked my son. I can take care of myself, he said. You're looking a lot better, by the way. That boosted my confidence, I took a walk to the shoe store. The clerk was on his lunch hour, I got tickets to a concert, I said, how about it? He took a look at my hairdo. Not bad, he said, I think I can make it. He picked me up at eight-thirty. We sat in the last row, spotted my son and the blonde a couple seats up. What do you make of that, I asked. He said you have to give them some slack, they come around in the end. We stopped for a drink on the way home. The kid never really had a father, I told him. I think it affected him. I could talk to him, he said, I have a couple boys of my own. You never told me, I said. What happened to their mother? He said it didn't work out, she expected too much. I invited him for supper the next night, told my son to bring the blonde.

Let's have coffee in the kitchen, I told her. I need some advice on my clothes. I sat by the door so I could listen. For starters that skirt's gotta go, she said. Tell me about your family, I said, do you live with your parents? She told me they threw her out when she was seventeen and in love. She wanted to talk to me about them sometime since we were about the same age. Spare me, I said, I have problems of my own. You mean your son, she said. Don't

worry, I haven't touched him. He's good looking but a little na-
ive. He misses his father. I do my best, I told her, but I'm not a
young woman. I could fix you up, she said. I know a lot of guys. I
said I liked the silent type. They were yelling in the living room.
Excuse me, I said, we better go in there. My son had the clerk by
the throat. It's my fault, I told him, I put him up to it. Don't be too
hard on him, the clerk said, I got a little overbearing. They shook
hands and I turned to the blonde. You really think this skirt's so
bad, I asked. She offered to take me shopping the next day.

I picked her up early, left a note for my son. When we got back
his clothes were gone. He went to live with his father, I told her,
I could see it coming. Ever think about getting a job, she asked. I
started working in the office building next to hers, we had lunch
every day. She brought in letters from my son, he was working on
a ranch near his father's place. Invite him for the holidays, I said,
he always liked the tree. He showed up with a girl his own age.
They announced their engagement that night. Are you the maid
of honor, I asked the blonde. He's pretty young, she said, but
they seem sensible. She helped me pick out a dress. I wondered
if the clerk would be my date. He'd be a fool to say no, the
blonde said, you look twenty years younger. I went to the wed-
ding on his arm. My husband said I looked matronly, I must be
working too hard. I approached a couple of old flames. You'll be
a grandmother soon, they said. It couldn't happen to a nicer person. I was disappointed and retired to the bathroom. The blonde
was in there combing her hair. I just don't have it anymore, I
said. I need a change of pace. That's no problem, she said, I have
relatives in the south who love to entertain.

I went home and packed. The blonde's sister was pretty home-
ly. I walked out to the garden where her husband was pruning
the roses. The best things in life are free, he told me. I should
have guessed something was up. I was just getting into bed
when he knocked at the door. My wife's a good cook but there's
more to life, he said. Don't you agree? I had a thing about southern gentlemen but I didn't want to rush it. Let's have some tea, I
said. I have to think this over. He bowed out gracefully. I decided to write to my daughter-in-law.

It's pretty hot down here, I wrote. If you
need advice I'm as close as the phone.

We had breakfast on the terrace. I described my husband's career. He was successful at first, I said, but people took advantage
of him. He could never say no to a lady. The brother-in-law
kissed my hand and suggested a drive to the lake. His wife said
she had a headache, so I excused myself and put on my best
dress. It had a coffee stain on the front but I hid it with my purse.
For the first hour we read magazines. He brought a big selection
and I tried to seem interested. Finally he looked up. I believe in
honesty, he said. Let's have an affair, my wife's used to it by now.
He said she liked to read, I should look at her library sometime.
I said I would, I wanted to avoid hurt feelings. He wasn't much
of a lover and I was glad to get back to the house. I discussed my
favorite author with his wife. We had a lot in common, and I
promised to write when I left the next week.

The first thing I did was look up the blonde. The school was
losing money and she was thinking of moving. What did you
think of him, she said. No offense, I said, but I pity your sister.
My son came home and his wife announced she was pregnant. I
asked her if she got my letter. I've been meaning to call you, she
said. He spends all his time in front of the mirror. Don't worry, I
said, it's a stage he'll outgrow. The blonde left town the next
day. I helped her load the car and thanked her for my new look. I
hope you find a husband, I said. She promised to keep in touch.
I got a card a month later, she was living with my son's father.
They were working a big spread, owned a hundred head of cat-
tle. How do you like that, I asked my son. He looked depressed
there in the mirror. I went to my bedroom, sat down at the desk.

We're still legally married, I wrote, half of
that is mine.

CAUGHT UP IN ROMANCE

We meet in my neighborhood restaurant. I pretend I don't see him, he's back from Europe and wearing a new suit. We both like to dance and stay out late that night. I introduce him to my family and they're all impressed. He isn't like my other boyfriends. I don't tell them about his business, make up something about textiles. It's the right thing to say and we spend a weekend at the cottage. He proposes after breakfast and we go on a whirlwind tour. I'm still a little shy but he doesn't expect me to talk. It isn't a bad life and I save a lot of money.

I don't like his associates, they're tall and drop in at odd hours. I listen from the bathroom but don't understand the language. My mother tells me not to worry, she didn't like my father's friends. Then his partner commits suicide. He seems to take it in stride but I start having nightmares. We go away for the weekend, I demand to know what's up. He says it's a long story, he's sure I'll get hysterical. Don't be silly, I tell him. He sits down on the couch and tells me his life story.

I was born in the Middle East, he says, my father was a merchant. When I was twelve there was an accident, I inherited the family business with my grandfather, a deranged old man. He was squandering everything, I had to grow up fast. I hid his body in the well, they still haven't found it. The old man's sister suspected me, tried to have me arrested. Luckily she was senile, I appealed to the government and they promised to protect me. I came to America, changed my identity. Whatever I do I owe them a cut.

I'm quiet for a long time. My father is in prison for back taxes. I know how it is to live on the run. I tell him about my savings, offer to share it with him in a new location. He sounds interested and says he'll talk to his banker in the morning. We make love all night and I'm glad I said something. We settle on South America. I pack up all my furs. My mother cries at the airport and I leave her a diamond watch. I know she'll miss my parties but there's nothing I can do. We rent a house by the water, my husband goes to town every morning but comes home for lunch. I don't ask what he's doing. I'm afraid for my father. The prime minister brings his mistress to dinner. We take a liking to each other, she's about my size and I borrow her clothes. She's attractive and knows the local men. I have chances for affairs but I'm the quiet type and not interested. One man keeps calling, I relent and we go for a walk. He looks something like my father, we talk about our childhoods. His father was a policeman in a small town, everyone knew his family. He took the mayor's daughter to the prom, they got engaged the next year. Two days later she was trampled by a horse, he never forgave himself. It was an act of God, I say. He feels human for the first time in years, we make a date for the next day.

I get tired of his attention. He's small and doesn't like to be seen in public. My husband's home every afternoon and I'm tired of the bedroom. I think about running away but a fight's coming up, my husband boxes and I have to make an appearance. I wear my best outfit, I want my husband to be proud. He's first on the schedule, I smile and look excited. He wins the first two rounds, gets knocked out in the third. We have a coke on his break and he can't take his eyes off me. Back in the ring he looks up at my seat, I yell at him to pay attention. It's too late and his ribs get broken. We're waiting for the ambulance when the police drive up, they have a warrant for his arrest. He's wanted for his partner's murder, they have the papers to send him back home. Down at the station he confesses. It wasn't suicide after all, he pushed him out the window. I was caught up in romance and never suspected. The police chief nods and goes to make a phone call. I'll stick by you, I say, we can make a new start. He talks to his lawyer and starts to look hopeful, then I mention my father. Sorry, the lawyer says, you'll have to divorce her. I resign myself, one prisoner in the family is enough.

COOKIE MUELLER

TOP STORIES   #19-20 $6.00

HOW TO GET RID OF PIMPLES

BY COOKIE MUELLER

HOW TO GET RID
OF PIMPLES

Here are the tales of woe,, the stories of the shunned, the biographies of the shy ones once scuttled to the darkest corners of any room. Looking in mirrors has always been a painful experience for these people and that's why I wrote this book. Even before this book was begun, I received letters asking for it, as it had already gotten some advance notice in John Waters' book Shock Value.

I was once a sufferer myself so I know well what the experience is like. The cure, that I discovered through many years of experimentation and correlation of already documented medical facts, changed my life. I suddenly liked myself.

While reading this book you may begin to wonder if it is something other than what the title indicates. It is not. The actual cure is in the back of the book, on the last pages. If you wish to skip the tales and go directly to the amazing cure, do it.

The following is a copy of one of the many letters I received a few years ago.

Dear Cookie,

Hi how are you doing? I just love you in
John's films. I just think you're wonderful.

I'm writing because I want to ask you how
you may get your booklet on How To Get
Rid of Pimples. I read about it in John's
book, Shock Value and I'd love to have
it.

I really don't have an acne problem but
it would be nice to have it on hand,
just in case.

Thanks a lot Cookie. I hope to be hearing
from you soon.

IOONA
THE THIRD TWIN

In a suburban house with white shingles and black shutters, Ioona, a woman of forty lived with her mother, a woman of sixty-four. The mother depended on her daughter now that she had emphysema and spent most of her time divided between lying in an oxygen tent surrounded by legions of waiting oxygen drums and being propped on pillows in the front window, overlooking the garden, on display to the neighbors.

That Ioona, back again with her mother after a fifteen year sojourn in a lonely marriage to a man that was wealthy (money amassed through a patented adjustment to a rachet wrench), was capable and independent enough to take on the responsibilities of the house and her mother's illness was questionable. But she had taken a mature stand to leave her husband and quit the ruse of love. If she could do that, she could do anything.

So now she was home again, planting flowers for her mother with the seeds that her mother had given her. A profusion of color all over the lawn was what the older lady desired but Ioona threw away all the seeds but Impatience, Bachelor's Buttons and Sweet William because these names were meaningful to Ioona who squeezed significance from everything.

She went to the shopping mall every day to escape the sound of breathing. In the mall, the music was a cradle and all the mannequins in the windows wore clothes as bland as puree. She found herself, like the rest of the people there, speaking in hushed tones in reverence to the mall; intoxicated by the sheer size and force of the steel and stone and glass and the endless displays of things to buy. But she wasn't very similar to these mall-goers at all. She was strong and fierce, despite the blue tablets of Librium she took four times a day to quell her feelings of insecurity. Unable to relax, always wanting new input or streamlined stimuli, she drove around at high speeds in her mother's beige Volare dreaming about transformation and destruction. Most often she dreamed of the Phoenix, living and burning, repeatedly rising from the flames and rubble of the shopping mall; wings spread, casting shadows on all of suburbia. When her dreams went flaccid and weren't enough, she thought about meeting a man and how she would do it.

One day at the mall she went into a bar, a place called Libby's Lounge. Her mother had warned her about this place as if there was something horribly off-color about it, but Ioona knew that her mother had probably never been in any bar in her entire life. It was exactly like any other; dark and carpeted and quiet in the day.

Ioona expected to meet a man there and she did. His name was William Way. When they began to talk and drink together in the coolness of the lounge she knew that finally she had met someone so much like herself that she felt almost as if miraculously her DNA double helix had uncoiled to make this man. Here was the man for her, someone who shared her every mood, someone who had been waiting just for her.

She brought him to her home and they fucked in her bedroom with the background noise of her mother's labored breathing and the oxygen whooshing from the tanks.

Whatever similarities that this new couple, Bill and Ioona, shared, the fact that Bill had been a Franciscan monk brought them the closest. In the fifteen years of abstinence and isolation with only his pets as companions, he gathered a certain knowledge of the natural world.

He stirred her into the initial sexual response by telling her about male kangaroos and opossums who have forked dicks, the females, forked vaginas. He told her about Abyssinian bats who have dicks with bristles just like bottle brushes.

He told her about the day he had taken a live mouse and carefully cut it open to take a cellular tissue scraping from the heart to see the tiny piece under the microscope pulsing all by itself. This fact made her see the order of life that before she had only dreamed was true. This monk . . . he was perfect.

They didn't marry but he moved in and together they buried her mother—only grudgingly had she relinquished her tenacious grasp on life. They planted tomatoes, corn and sunflowers where all the flowers had been. In the summer they took his boat to the edge of the falls and in autumn they burned leaves on the front lawn. In winter, they went out on the frozen river to cut holes in the ice and fish.

One day on the ice the ex-monk fell into one of the holes and when he finally bobbed up, he was in a cube of ice and dead.

And now Ioona buried him alone and wanted to leave her body but didn't have the courage to commit suicide nor the patience to coax astral travel by meditation. Then she found out that she was pregnant and there was someone else, a third twin perhaps, within her thinking all those wonderful uterine thoughts. She was consoled. This really was just the beginning and she was finally after all these years being included into life's mysterious order where tranquility's sweet bloodless arms would envelope her and rock her until the end.

THE CIRCUMSTANCES OF IOONA'S CURE

It goes without saying that one would be surprised to find a woman of forty with acne. It is so often associated with adolescence. When a woman of forty gets pregnant for the first time the hormones go haywire.

Ioona got pimples. She came to me and I gave her the cure. By the time she was five months pregnant there weren't any pimples. The cure not only cleared her skin but strengthened her and her baby who turned out to be a girl . . . an amazing child.

Ioona remarried later to a man who was pretty fat and boy was he a happy man. They had a son a year later and the husband/father was so happy that he laughed so loud he shook the house. He was also a very lucky man to have found Ioona.

What is the function of all of these single-sentence deaths and marriages?

Ideas of strength and weakness. Strong enough to leave first husband, not strong enough to commit suicide. Needs new husband in real-bad. Humorously tragic! Does last movement make transition into pimples more acceptable?

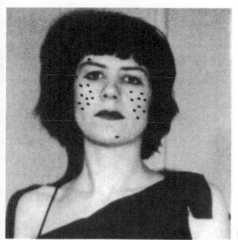

Before

After

GODA

Goda could not look in the mirror and see herself. Because her hair was ashen, her eyes pale grey and her skin the color of aluminum, she did not reflect well in the glass. There were pimples and even these were silver but they stood out sorely.

Her image, as she perceived it, wavered from opaque to translucent to non-existent. She thought perhaps that she could pass through walls or doors or eavesdrop on relevant conversations without her presence being noticed, but she could do none of these things. Even when her form was invisible and she was sure she wasn't seen, people would feel her as a phantom. Perhaps it would be a slight itch on the back of the neck of a person deep in verbal intercourse with business partners. Another would shoo away a fictive fly, yet another would keep turning to see if there was something or someone beside him. But there was no one and there was nothing. She would walk into a room without legs and feet and footsteps but still there wasn't a person who didn't glance towards her. She couldn't walk down the street and melt all the way.

It was a strange doublet, this duo association of unsubstantiality and entity. She felt the tug from both sides. It became impossible to believe in herself.

Goda went out late at night to clubs where she thought people might see her. Men and women with cameras took pictures of her for no reason and the pictures would sometimes appear in night-life magazines, but her image would always be missing. In one particular magazine called Nightblind she saw the two men she had been standing between and there was a blank space where she was supposed to be. So where was she? For sure she had been there. She remembered that George had been drinking the Beck's and David had been drinking the Remy Martin. She even remembered what she had been drinking. A smart cocktail. A martini. But where was she? Could she have been mistaken? Maybe the art editor airbrushed her image because of the pimples? But they wouldn't have done that. No. She just didn't show up because her form was as silver as the photographic plates.

She may well have not shown up in photos but she had a life. There were people who called her on the phone and certainly they asked for her by name.

"Could I speak to Goda?" they would ask.

Or they would say, "Is Goda there?"

She was there alright.

"I must be here ... there are people asking for me," she would say to herself often.

From time to time she would go out on dates with people and they would talk at the table over the candle cup while eating Japanese, Chinese, Italian, Indian, Thai or Polish food, depending on what type of restaurant they went to. The person would look directly into her eyes so naturally, she thought for sure she must have been there, otherwise they would be alone and reading a newspaper. Right?

She decided that her problem must be stemming from the dilemma of the pimples. She had them since she was sixteen and now she was twenty-six and they weren't getting any better.

Perhaps it would be more agreeable to be a newspaper but then she would inevitably be folded up like a daily and left on a seat somewhere on a bus or in a restaurant.

All that mattered were the pimples. Her nose didn't matter, or her eyes or her wide smile. It was only the pimples. She would have squeezed them or applied Clearisil or alcohol if she could have found her image in her bathroom mirror.

She began to consider throwing in the towel, but it was then that she found the answer.

THE CIRCUMSTANCES OF GODA'S CURE

One day she called me. She had heard. I had never seen her before. She asked me for the cure and I gave it to her. She followed my advice. Two months later she called me back. I never saw her. From the sound of her voice I could tell something had changed, she was different. Before, her voice sounded like shards in a wastepaper basket, a voice that sounded like the head behind it believed it held no future rewards; bleached out, bleeding white. Now the voice was effusive and cheerful.

She told me that because of my cure, she no longer had any pimples, not even a greyhead. She was happy. Now she would appear in night life magazines and there would be her image in black and white or color. She could even see herself in shades of grey.

Before

After

Photo © 1984 Peter Hujar

JOE

What remained of Joe was sitting on Janie's mantlepiece in a yellowish marble urn. Yellow had been his favorite color. Joe had wanted to be burned and often said he thought that undertakers weren't very honest and they would keep the dead person's pants and shoes for themselves because that part of the deceased was never on display in the coffin. Joe didn't like to think of his favorite shoes on anyone else. *feel cheated when have nothing to look at—previous passage?*

Everyone, all of Joe's children, sisters, brothers, past and present wives and lovers felt very cheated. They didn't understand cremation. There was nothing to look at during the eulogy, only the urn and a four by six foot color photograph of him at the morgue, dead but smiling. The picture was his present wife Janie's idea and she did it to satisfy those with little imagination. *images needed for those with little imagination?*

The funeral group got out of hand . . . everyone wanted something more, so Janie, always diplomatic, got out a huge mirror and dumped the entire contents . . . every bit of Joe's ashes onto it and divided it up with a razor blade. Obviously Janie did it partly for effect. She was angry at their callous behavior so she thought she may as well shock them by way of example. *drug imagery*

The guests were aghast but enthusiastically brought out containers like envelopes and pill vials to put their portions in. Joe's agent wanted a larger amount. He always had wanted a larger piece of Joe. *happen to Cur program?*

At one time Joe worked as a TV sitcom writer but toward the end of his life, wrote the material for a famous comedian who had always trod the line between political satire and fearless celebrity putdowns. He told audiences just what was on his mind. He spared no one.

One day a dissident stood up in the audience. People in seats behind him told him to "siddown asshole" but he pulled from his pocket a .38. Without the look to anger or insanity, without a word of warning, he fired a shot at he comedian but missed him. The bullet went past him and hit Joe who was waiting backstage holding revised scripts. That's how Joe died. It was quick.

When the murderer was told who he had really killed he said on nationwide TV that he was happier that he had hit the writer because the comedian was just the figurehead anyway.

Joe, all bloodied up, had to laugh in spite of his wound and he laughed so hard about the irony, that he still had a smile on his lips when they wheeled him into the morgue and took that last picture.

Janie, who knew everything about Joe, couldn't grieve too much. Joe said often that he wanted to go by an assassin's bullet. She knew he wasn't joking about it, because it was the quickest way for a writer of his stature to become immortal.

So Joe really wasn't gone. He would live on and on, riding on the air waves. As a TV sitcom writer there had been only a handful of equals. Everybody knows that until the end of time there will always be re-runs.

[handwritten margin left: time → echoes — became furious]

[handwritten below paragraph: by hurting ppl. and there-by being hurt himself.]

THE CIRCUMSTANCES OF JOE'S CURE

Joe always told me that when comedy writers died they wouldn't go to heaven . . . the place was too boring . . . not a good time. On their way to hell the oarsman on the River Styx would laugh so much at their jokes that he wouldn't have the heart to deliver them to hell.

When I asked him why he didn't think these people would go to heaven he said something like this: "The ability to take a sad situation, instantly access and glean its potential sight gag or one-liner virtues, then turn it into something that would make someone laugh, is sort of perverted. Perverted people don't go to heaven." *[handwritten: All of these people have each something perverted]*

As a young man Joe had problem skin and this he used to joke about. After he followed my cure and had great skin, the cure was the butt of the jokes. Then I was the butt of the jokes. Then he would joke about clear skin. Everything was a joke. He didn't know how to enjoy or appreciate a good old morbid or horrible moment without turning it into something funny.

[handwritten right margin: and anyway. What is funny? Something.]

[handwritten bottom: this seems to be what Mueller is doing as well.]

Before

After

Photo ©1984 David Armstrong

[handwritten: coloration again ↑]   **DORA**   *[handwritten: after strangely colored girl is a model]*

Through Dora's veins ran the cold purple blood that gave her hair and eyes a pale eggplant tinge. Despite such an obvious mark of bearing, she was rarely recognized as an aristocrat. She was always being lumped into the same gene pool as the rest of them, the unremarkable middle-of-the-roaders, the average, the mediocre. No one knew that she thought of herself as a philanthropist, perhaps most people who knew her wouldn't even realize that there was such a word in the English language. Her benevolence to the masses made her pursue things like bartending and go-go dancing. Four nights a week she worked at Joe Protozoa's after-hours place where she stood behind a make-shift fiberglass bar looking not unlike an objet d'art misplaced in a swine barn.

The surface of the bar was all pitted from the stiffness of the drinks she slammed down. One could always smell rancid cigarette-butts, mature sponges, sour booze and human mildew. An electric air freshener hummed, laboring foolishly, impervious to the impossibility of the task, yet at the same time it added another veneer of cheapness to the already impoverished smell of it all. Even without lights one would guess that the place looked awful and it did.

The drinkers who came in mostly drank it neat. They were usually alone and wide awake. Every single one of them would tell her in greatest detail each moment of their sordid existences. She was very kind, but never opened herself up to them; she was the voyeur and recorded in a diary she called *The Monster With Many Heads* every word they told her in conversation. She felt compelled to do this for some reason, perhaps it was because she thought she was doing charity work, that these people needed some kind of inner healing. As a go-go dancer in other bars she had danced her way into many a sick heart because she suspected in their flaccid brains she represented a human tonic that cured paranoia, melancholia, loneliness, misery. All the amounts of gold chains and diamond pinky rings that flashed in the lights of the mirrored disco balls couldn't hide the fact that these people were bankrupt, not financially, but emotionally and culturally. All the capped teeth and hairpieces belied their broken bodies. Most

[handwritten left margin: what the simple curl clues! Because girls negativity throughout - lack of whimsy on part - lack of wonders in life]

154

of the people in the after-hours bar were thieves, boosters, pimps, porno moguls, hit men, numbers runners, coke dealers, but most of them were ordinary liars, so who could know the truth. Maybe they were just trying to look more powerful than they were. One thing was for sure, they were all drawn together by one common affliction: the desire to stay bombed until noon.

One particular morning was completely different than any other she had known. Dora felt odd, not bad, but she noticed that she was kind of glowing, she felt big, as big as the world.

When a thief named Ian came in and told her of how he ripped a man off after he picked him up at a hustlers' bar, Dora didn't exactly upbraid him but when Ian left the bar he was going straight to the man's house where he had stolen the money and the jewelry to return it. She had made him feel unclean about it. She wasn't sure of how she had done it, it certainly wasn't planned.

A junkie named Mary came in a little later and Dora somehow convinced Mary that she ought to quit using the drug. Mary left the place determined to go straight to Narcotics Anonymous that day. Dora was shining bluish white, her illumination shining bluish white, her illumination was falling on everybody that walked in. Even Frank, the bouncer who frisked people for weapons at the door noticed it.

Around 6 a man came into the bar and placed himself in front of her. He told her his name was Delicious and he'd had the flu for three months and he couldn't shake it.

"I'm on fire," he said, "I'm burning up with fever."

Dora placed her right hand on his black forehead. He was very hot. She tried to remove her hand but there was something there that wouldn't allow that. Her hand stuck like a pin to a magnet. When the pull relaxed she withdrew her hand and the big black handsome man Delicious shuddered.

"I don't feel hot anymore. Did you feel something strange? It was like you took this fire into your hands. Girl, you got some healing hands. What the hell is it? You a saint or something?" he was visibly shaken and aghast.

Dora shrugged her shoulders and looked at her hand.

"I don't know," she said, "I don't know."

Two minutes later a man came in and ordered a Harvey's Bristol

Cream on ice. He told her that he'd just had a fourteen pound cancerous tumor removed and he still couldn't walk properly. In fact, he was doubled over on his stool. He told her also that the prognosis wasn't good, the doctors didn't feel that they'd gotten all the cancer and that he didn't have a long time to live, they guessed.

When Dora took the money from him, their hands met for a moment and they stuck like cement. Both of them looked down at their hands in fear. When the tug was over the man straightened up in his seat.

"It's gone. I feel it's gone." He stood up. "I don't feel no nausea no more. I can walk. I'm cured."

People came in all morning until 10 a.m. with physical problems and she unwittingly helped them. She had no idea of what was happening. The place was packed with Dora worshippers. They wouldn't leave, even when the place was closing up. Frank had to escort her home. They all wanted to touch her.

Soon word spread that there was a healer at Joe Protozoa's. They said that Dora walked with the angels. From that morning on the place was crowded with unfortunates of every kind; the blind, the poor, the overworked, the crippled, the insane. There were more people waiting on line at Joe Protozoa's than there were at Lourdes in France.

Joe Protozoa was raking in the bucks but he was afraid of the police. After all, these kinds of bars didn't need a lot of publicity. Liquor was against the law after 4 a.m.

He had to hire doormen and used velvet ropes to keep out the people who were in good shape. Only the obvious sick and crippled or suffering person could enter the place. Of course, there were always a few people who feigned disease or faked a limp or dressed like the insane but the doormen were astute and the phonies rarely got as far as the coat check room.

"Nobody is getting in unless you got something wrong with you," Frank the bouncer said over and over.

People on stretchers got in first. Party people looking for the action were turned away.

"Come back when there's something wrong with ya," Frank would say.

Of course Dora got a cut of the money and so did the cops to keep their mouths shut. A few months later when Dora was hailed as a saint, the beatified bartender, and TV crews had interviewed her, politicians wanted her in their camps, churches rallied for her attentions, she discovered that she was in danger. Her life was being threatened by the A.M.A. In the United States illness was a big money-making business. Without sick people whole industries would starve, the whole economy of the United States was in danger with Dora around.

She left the country in a veil with phony passports from the thieves at Joe's. She went to a leper colony in the Pacific and cured the lepers there, she went to hospitals in India and made the sick well.

Little did she know that a C.I.A. man was following her all over the world. He went to the leper colony and to India.

When she came back into the country in a disguise, he followed her here. She was longing to see her parents and her friends at Joe's. She never left J.F.K. airport. The C.I.A. man got to her first and calmly wiped her out.

It was a routine murder condoned by the government, blessed by the A.M.A. Alas, this always happens to the real saints. What else would one expect?

For his ghastly deed the C.I.A. man contracted leprosy from his trip to the Pacific and he longed for Dora to be alive again to cure him. Other than this, there was no punishment for the death of Dora. The C.I.A. and the A.M.A. weren't really proud of themselves but what else could they have done? It was out of their hands. They didn't blame themselves for one minute, it was God's fault they said, she was born at the wrong time. If only she could have been born before there was an A.M.A., then everything would have been rosy. Oh well.

THE CIRCUMSTANCES OF DORA'S CURE

The A.M.A. doesn't like me either, but they wouldn't bother to kill me, there's too many of them with rotten skin.

Dora was one of my patients many years ago. She was the first. My cure worked well on her. Could you imagine a saint with acne?

Before

After

THE ACTUAL CURE

Have you heard enough? I could tell you more endless depressing tales of people with bad skin but I won't. I'm going to get right to the facts. The cure is simple and it isn't expensive or time consuming. I'm not selling a product. All the things you'll need are already on your kitchen shelf or at the drug store or health food store.

Through trial and error and a lot of research I've cured myself of acne. I've cured many people who have religiously followed my program. This cure works. This is not a joke.

O.K. Here goes.

If you have bad skin you have a vitamin A and D deficiency. The most readily digestible form of these vitamins are contained in cod liver, halibut liver and shark liver oil. I take cod liver oil, two tablespoons a day. To many people the taste is very disagreeable. If this is the case there are perls (gelatine capsules) of these oils which can be taken. The cod liver oil I take is 2500 I.U.s (International Units) of vitamin A and 250 I.U.s of vitamin D per gram. There are water misible pills as well, these are the dry form of the vitamins. I suggest taking the oil misible form of these vitamins.

There is caution to be noted when taking vitamin A. There is a toxicity level of this vitamin so don't take more than 50,000 I.U.s daily. Research has shown that the body can't utilize more than this anyway.

If you've had bad skin for a number of years, you might have noticed that exposure to the sun tends to clear up the problem. The sun gives you vitamin D. There is a type of cholesterol present in the skin that the sun's ultraviolet rays activate, converting it to vitamin D. This vitamin also aids in the absorption of calcium, which acne sufferers are also deficient in. Don't overdo the sun though, because the tanner and thicker your skin becomes, the less vitamin D your skin absorbs. A deficiency of vitamin D leads to retention of phosphorus in the kidneys and there is a relationship to proper kidney functioning and healthy skin.

Vitamin E is also essential to the cure. Vitamin E is an antioxidant which means it prevents saturated fatty acids from breaking down and combining with other substances that might become harmful to the body. Vitamin E has the ability to unite with oxygen thus the red blood cells are more fully supplied with pure oxygen that the heart and other organs obviously need. Vitamin E is effective in the prevention of scarring on the body surface and internally. It can be used to prevent calcification of the kidneys.

You should take 200 to 400 I.U.s of vitamin E daily.

The B complex vitamins should not be ignored. They help reduce facial oiliness and blackhead formation. B vitamins are the single most important factor for health of the nerves and proper functioning of the nervous system. It is proven that emotional stress and nervousness contribute to acne problems. The best way to get the B complex is Brewer's Yeast. It contains 40% highest quality protein and is an excellent source of most minerals and trace elements. It contains 16 amino acids. Amino acids are the basic units of digested protein.

Many people can't tolerate the taste of Brewer's Yeast, so instead a high poten-cy vitamin B complex pill should be taken. Never take just one or two of the Bs alone, an improper balance of these vitamins is not beneficial.

Vitamin C should be included with the B vitamins because it activates them. Also it aids in the resistance of the spread of acne infection.

Zinc gluconate (30 mg. daily), niacin (100 taken twice daily) and cold pressed oil (soy bean, sesame; one tablespoon daily) should be included.

As an adolescent I was always told to stay away from chocolate because it sup-posedly was bad for the skin. There is some truth in this. Chocolate, spinach and rhubarb inhibit the body's absorption of calcium because they contain an excess of oxalic acid. Oxalic acid can form kidney stones and kidney malfunctioning is always associated with skin problems. Calcium helps to maintain the acid alkali balance of the blood which is important for clear skin.

Avoid constipation, get plenty of sleep and exercise and try for peace of mind. Avoid an excess of animal fats in the diet. Take a natural multi-mineral formula and drink water, preferably mineral water. All of these dietary considerations are not so difficult to follow.

Now that you know what to do for the internal, here's what to do topically.

The most important consideration externally is to maintain a low pH acid man-tle on the skin. Wash with an acid balanced soap as opposed to an alkali one. The pH level should be 4.5 or lower. Without the proper acid mantle the skin is open for all kinds of bacteria and infections. To insure this protection you must rinse your face after every washing with a solution of apple cider vinegar and water, one part apple cider vinegar to four or five parts water.

Everything that you put on your face (if you use foundations etc.) should be acid instead of alkaline. You can buy little testing papers at the pharmacy called Nitrazine papers. The papers are yellow. If you test your facial products with these and the products turn the papers blue or purple then don't use these prod-ucts. They are too alkaline.

This apple cider vinegar and water solution is an essential part of the cure. You have to do it.

The routine is this: Apply a pure coconut or vitamin E oil on your face. You can also use the cod liver oil if you can stand the smell, then wash your face with hot water and the pH balanced soap, then rinse with water and follow it with the apple cider vinegar and water solution. If you feel that your skin is really too oily omit the first step.

If you follow all the directions I have cited here, the external and internal, you will notice that your skin will begin to clear up in a matter of two weeks. In six weeks your skin may begin to break out again. This is the time when all the tox-ins are being released. Don't get discouraged at this time, continue the program. The next week your skin will clear up for good. Old scars will even disappear! You must keep it up, don't stop. Whenever I do, I have a recurrence of acne. Do it. It works.

So that's the cure. It hasn't failed for anyone who's followed it. It has changed people's lives. To encapsulate:

Internal:
Vitamins A and D, always taken together as an oil (cod liver, halibut liver or shark liver, two tablespoons daily, not to exceed four)
A- 5,000 to 15,000 I.U.s daily, taken in a perl
D- 500 to 1,500 I.U.s daily, taken in a perl
B- taken as Brewer's Yeast, three heaping tablespoons daily
B complex in pill form - 20 to 100 mgs. daily for each B
C- 1,000 mgs. daily
E- 200 to 400 I.U.s daily
Zinc- 30 mgs. daily
Niacin- 100 mgs. twice a day (Don't take this if you're taking the Bs as Brewer's Yeast.)
Cold pressed oil-soybean, sesame, 1 tablespoon daily.

Avoid chocolate, spinach, rhubarb

External:
Wash with the pH balanced soap, rinse with hot water, followed by the apple cider vinegar solution; use pH balanced products.

So you see this isn't very difficult. This does work. For sure. So do it.

COOKIE

What is the function of the photos?
Why is the acne drawn on?
Do you think the story works and is cohesive?
Why is there no before picture of Cookie?

After

Photo © 1984 David Armstrong

162

ASCHER/STRAUS

RED MOON/RED LAKE

TOP STORIES   #21 $3.00

RED MOON/

RED LAKE

ASCHER/STRAUS

RED MOON/RED LAKE

Pam is asleep, the lavender cover just under her chin.

Her fingers or her eyelids may have moved a little, but the disposition of her body doesn't change. A hand that begins the night curled like a glove 1¾" from the pillow will crawl no further than 2" from the pillow by morning; the left ankle will remain tucked under the right calf. A body that seems to lack the vitality to transmit its dreams beyond a tiny envelope of warmth.

The room is covered over and dozing in a cool midnight blue shadow, exactly the same weight and temperature as the white powder blowing in thin clouds from large sacks of plaster stacked in rows on the parched slope of a lawn, below a high wall of loose yellow bricks and warped window frames.

Ted's made a nest for himself and his loose, dark bathrobe in the deep chair near the red oval rug, the small, leather-surfaced telephone table and the color television console. The television is on and in that sense it's true but not completely true, or true but also not true, or true in an utterly new way, that Ted is in the living room, nesting in the deep chair. It could be said just as truthfully that Ted is absolutely nowhere: the television, flashing a blue wash of pictures and a multitudinous blather of voices, is a second head, displacing Ted's as thoroughly as if his throat had been slit, his body hung by the feet from a rafter and drained of all its blood by the eight foot tall, human-like vegetable from outer space in *The Thing*. It's also possible that he's there, but also somewhere else: not totally displaced by the television's objective dreaming, but in an intermediate state of here and there, his photons annihilated in the television's.

The television is beaming a face close to Ted's. Montgomery Clift's narrow, troubled face, eyebrows darkened by guilt, ambitions, ethics, longings is gazing at Elizabeth Taylor, young and lovely, no more than nineteen or twenty. She's just taken a cold swim in the beautiful, dark lake and now she's towelling off her hair and laughing—the dark, shimmering laughter of a girl who's affectionate, happy and rich. A loon flies up from the surface of the lake, passes overhead, and disappears beyond the forest screen. Ted's face, at first next to Elizabeth Taylor's, finds itself next to Clift's, resting on his shoulder, extraordinarily close to the camera, a soft, untroubled pearl, the eyes and eyelashes dark with a sensual knowledge that seems to have something to do with the past and future secrets of the lake. A world of grace and freedom is breathing against Montgomery Clift's shadows.

Someone who's actually leaning on his windowsill on this autumn night is dozing and dreaming he's leaning on the windowsill on a summer night. A thin, dark-haired man of thirty-three who used to live in an orange brick house across the way, but who's now in an ancient, red brick hospital in a distant zone of the city. In a lucid moment he dreams that he's home, staring out his bedroom window and thinking: "if lucidity, heightened to its extreme, resembles dreams, then all I'm suffering from is a delirium of lucidity!" He sees a familiar, curly-haired neighbor in a near-distant window, leaning on the sill and staring at the moon.

The moon is a dark orange, with three still darker areas of blue shadow.

Dogs are barking, crying, baying at widely scattered points within a shallow basin that forms an uneven sound horizon. Leaning on the windowsills, the two men can hear the smothered voices of three dogs, then seven, locked in basements, kitchens or outdoor sheds, as unhappy as children who cry until they're exhausted, their mothers can't comfort them, no matter what. Or they cry until the moon is only a few inches above the dusky lavender of the roofs.

The moon is red now. Its blue shadows so dark they're like holes where they can see the moon's other sky.

The earth is moving perceptibly up across its surface: they can measure the movement, feel themselves being thrust upward and backward. The horizontal line of a television aerial atop the slate roof of the dark brick house across the way slides toward the moon's upper rim.

Now the moon's red is the deep red of the molten core of the planet: a round X-ray mirror deep in space. The two men, terror-stricken, withdraw into their rooms.

Ted is awake. Montgomery Clift has long since discovered that he's guilty, that, accident or no accident, he really wanted Shelly Winters to drown in the dark lake, and the 25" Zenith is broadcasting a coded program of dots and static.

All Ted remembers is that he's had another nightmare, one with a red overtone. He's seen The Butcher again or he's been butchered. The Butcher's shop looked like an enormous public toilet. Dismembered torsos lay in the toilet stalls, cranberry red. He struggles to remember more. It seems to him the nightmare began on a train. He remembers very rapid movement, a complex motion that involves swaying from side to side, vertical dipping and tremors, all the while standing still yet hurtling forward. The conductor insisted he make a decision at once: the crowded car near at hand or the empty one in the extreme distance. A long difficult journey: loss of balance; many many doors, hard to open. Arriving at the distant car, he felt as if he were at the bottom of a steep plane, as if horizontal and vertical had changed places. He slid back the door with great effort and saw: the slaughterhouse-toilet. He recognized it as the place he's been visiting ever since

Pam's enormous brother Rudi has been living in the tiny nursery just the other side of their bedroom wall.

Pam and Ted and Rudi are having supper together.

Pam is saying that there's a woman at work, just about her age, who was a language major just like her. Only it was French instead of German and the University of Wisconsin instead of Sacramento. Since this woman graduated she's worked at secretarial jobs exactly like the one she has now. First in Milwaukee, then Denver, Los Angeles, and now in New York. All on the same low level. The job in Los Angeles made a *little* use of her training in French, but not much. So, naturally, she's a little depressed.

Ted says: "What's there to be depressed about? Everybody works on a low level—and nobody makes use of anything. Two guys were talking on the beach the other night about that very thing. One of them said: 'you know what I've discovered? Every grey hair means something new you've forgotten. The secret of life is forgetfulness. Remembering is unnatural, that's why it takes so much effort. We're meant to get dumber and dumber with every day. Until, at the end. . . .' Actually, Rudi heard more of it than I did. Didn'tcha, Rudi?"

"More parsnips, please, Pam." Rudi has his thick hand out.

"Since I've been taking these walks with Rudi, I've developed a new ability. *Two* new abilities. I can hear what other people are saying. And I can *repeat* it."

"Even when you don't understand it," Rudi says.

Ted and Rudi laugh.

"Hey! I'm real happy *you* guys know what you're talkin' about—but I wish somebody'd *translate* or something. . . ."

More dishing out and eating, then Pam says: "Does anyone want to hear more about Penny?"

"Penny? Who's Penny?"

"The woman I was talking about, Ted!"

"Oh sure. . . ."

"Sure!"

"Well, *I* feel sympathetic even if you two don't."

"We're sympathetic. Aren't we, Rudi? We even *look* sympathetic. And that's worth more than anything."

"I'm really listening, Pam."

"Cause I'd like your serious opinion on this. I'm so darn na-ive—or so *optimistic*—that I think when someone's *down* like that it sort of skips right past me. I *wanted* to give her good advice, but I couldn't. For example: I don't at all understand what this means: 'If you don't decide, it decides for you. You think life is waiting for you to figure out what you want to do. But it doesn't wait. It goes on without your consent.' I said: 'Why do you have to know what you want to do? Look at me: I didn't *plan* the life I'm leading. It just happened. And *I'm* sure happy it worked out that way.' So Penny said: 'Is twenty-eight old or young?' so I said: 'Well. I'm twenty-eight—so I think it's *young*. I can still do anything. *You* can still do anything. People start careers *much* later than that.' 'Sometimes I think it's very old. Because the way things are, by twenty-eight you *must know what you're doing*. Or rather *you must already be doing it.*' I said: 'That's the wrong way to look at it.' So Penny said: 'Oh I can look at it the other way! Twenty-eight is *very* young—because I have so many years left to be unhappy. A whole life ahead of me to suffer. Poverty and lousy jobs and stupid relationships.' I suppose I got a little impatient, because I said: 'Well, gee, Penny, if we looked at life that way, we'd all go out and commit *suicide.*'"

Ted says: "I'm trying to remember who I met in the bakery yesterday who made me think—'sometimes a person harbors grudges you know nothing about. You meet someone you haven't seen for a year and you find out he's been hating you for a long time. . . .'"

Rudi says: "She isn't telling you the truth, Pam."

Ted stops carving his boiled beef and Pam lays down her forkful of cabbage.

"Who isn't telling me the truth, Rudi? You guys'v got me confused! Are you talking about someone in the bakery now or what . . . ?"

"This woman Penny is lying to you. She's only telling you the part you want to hear. She *knows* you were a language major and that you're too intelligent for the job you're doing. She knows you only pretend to like it. She might even know you took a stupid, low-paying job just to make Ted feel better about the stupid, low-paying job *he* has. People know things, Pam. She told you a little—and then she saw that it bothered you—that you were dumb enough or just unhappy enough to think you were like her. So she told you a little more. But she *didn't* tell you the part that would have made you realize you were different. She didn't tell you that she had a breakdown while she was in Denver. And that all through the months in the hospital she couldn't do the simplest things. She couldn't even cut out a leather book mark in arts and crafts. She wasn't released from the hospital in Denver. She slipped out and went to Los Angeles. Her mother's been in one mental hospital or another for fifteen years. Penny and her older sister, Gloria, grew up in foster homes. The father's alive, but he's crazy too. Weighs more than I do—mean and sloppy—lives without heat or electricity in a house full of old tires and automotive parts. Penny and Gloria were very close until Gloria got married, had children. Now Penny has no one. Last year she had an abortion and wanted to stay with her sister, but for some reason Gloria was furious about the whole thing and they haven't spoken since. Penny's latest boyfriend is a Howard Johnson's waiter. He's crazy too. The morning she talked to you she dreamed that she and her boyfriend stabbed somebody who looked like her father. Her mother was upset because they got blood on the carpet. So she had to clean it up. She washed the body and scrubbed the rug. Then the father came back to life and was sitting in a chair. The mother was hiding in a closet and her boyfriend got slashed. Then there was something about a body in the grandfather clock—and another part where she and her boyfriend were checking each other in the bathroom. She was putting a bandage on his wound and he was examining her body. He was touching her intimately. She started to feel aroused and woke up. So, in many ways, Pam, I think Ted has much more in common with Penny than you do. Ted doesn't think so, and nobody else might think so, except his kid sister, Betty, but I think his parents belong in an institution."

Ted says Pam can't be like Penny because Pam has no dream life at all.

Rudi says Ted is wrong, Pam dreams about old age. And she dreams about Granma Rich's grape arbor in Arkansas, just the way he does. Her grape arbor and her money. Pam knows and he knows and Polly may know too how many hundreds of thousands Granma Rich has socked away down there. Thirty, forty, maybe fifty years of usury. One of these days they'll find her with an ax head in her brain pan.

Pam says she just realized how insane it was to make boiled beef at this time of year.

Some time after midnight.

Exactly the same midnight all along the street, or each second just a little bit different with every inch of distance.

The moon, unusually dark and orange, almost red, splits the sky into two distinct sections, one of them a bit bluer than the other, as if composed of fewer and more transparent layers. In that part of the sky something is shining. There something is approaching. Something as enormous and brilliant as daylight is going to show its face.

No one sees the enormous figure standing on the porch of the house with the white frame first story, red frame upper stories, one finger deep in the bell socket. He stands flat against the wall next to the door, as if waiting for someone to make the mistake of coming down to have a look around.

A window opens on the second floor, a withered face with a limp halo of red-in-black or black-in-red curls gazes out attentively at the slowly developing photograph of the street, listens acutely to the thin band of sound along the horizon, one, two, three sharp cries in the foreground. Sees no one; hears nothing or does hear something subaudible, human breathing that might also be wind in hemlock saplings; closes the window and recedes from dark window surface to dark bed. A broad white shirt sails down the street, unseen or seen only by the eyes of children awakened by nightmares.

The rain that's falling at 5 am is so fine it's little more than heavy mist.

The streetlamps haven't gone off yet. And wherever there's a streetlamp the atmosphere looks even bluer than it is.

The streetlamps along the boardwalk that frames the ocean as a repetitive sequence of horizontal vistas are placed with the utmost regularity. Between the broad cones of odd, daylight pink, there are slight, marginal spaces of natural light where one can see that the sun may already have risen in a luminous sky.

A guy in a hemp-colored shirt and dark trousers, who's been sitting on a bench, drinking beer and getting wet, is staggering down the wooden ramp, cradling a brown paper supermarket sack. Seven-hundred-and-twelve steps down from the ramp he passes one of the channels where darkness is running between the houses. Ten empty Budweiser cans make a tremendous clatter on the sidewalk, two full cans roll out of the dark, across the sidewalk, down the shallow driveway grade.

Across the way a white lace curtain behind a closed window is twitching as if the window were open. Someone, agitated, isn't certain if she's seen something odd. Where can the man have disappeared to? She knows for sure that he doesn't live anywhere in that row of two-family, treeless houses, neither modern nor anything else, an absolute architectural dead point whose inhabitants every morning shake off a wierdly pleasing neutrality in order to accomplish the tasks of the day. He always follows a path, as if avoiding invisible obstacles, toward the old-rice-colored apartment building on the boulevard. The impression that he'd been jerked obliquely, slightly upward, like someone launching into a difficult backward dive, is already beginning to break down into more conventional possibilities. She notices that a few tiny, beet-colored leaves and blue flowers have popped up overnight on her lawn. The blue of the tiny flowers absorbs all her attention: the blue of a distant land mass, perhaps the coast of New Jersey, visible across how many surface miles of ocean, with all its deep shadows and superficial whirlpools.

A few twigs of sunlight appear for the first time through a dark, scattered fleet of morning clouds.

A hedge is built up rapidly, yellow as wicker.

A hedge and then hedges.

Along the boardwalk several apartment houses are reconstructing themselves brick by brick out of a moist and gleaming sunlight.

When the sun touches the greenish blinds of a sixth story window sparks pass across 5×10^{23} gaps and the engine of the day starts up.

Sunshine on the waxed wood floor and the bright red rug: the tv set translating comic forces into pictures of Buddy Ebson shooting and being shot at in a dark parking garage: the panes white with sunlight. Rudi is sitting on the coral convertible couch, reading last week's *Sunday News* and chuckling while Pam fixes dinner and Ted repairs a lamp cord.

"Did you get a nice letter from your Mom, honey? Did she have anything interesting to say?"

"I haven't opened it yet."

"But you got it on Friday, honey. Aren't you at all curious about what your Mom's life is like in Vegas?"

Ted's answer is inaudible.

"Well, I guess I'll put the spaghetti up."

"Terrific."

"Let Pam read the letter, Ted," Rudi says from the couch without looking up from the paper.

"Oh Teddy! *Could* I? Would it be alright? Can I read the letter while you do that? Oh, Ted, I love you!"

Dear Pam & Ted,

A happy, healthy and prosperous first anniversary. I am fine. I took it very easy this week. Like everybody else, tired and broke. So I took a good rest on Saturday and then again today. Besides, we've had unusually cold weather here. Freezing—every-one down here thinks it's freezing—till today. And when it's windy it does feel a little like New York. Many people are sick. Thank God I'm fine. Enjoyed a walk in the beautiful Nevada sun today—by the orange wall and the tremendous eucalyptus trees. Am now getting my hair done.

Thank you so much for the Hummel music box. The "Merry Widow" Waltz. My favorite song! And when it gets too quiet in the apartment I play it. Though it's always noisy at the club and music, such as it is, constantly. So I really enjoy the peace and quiet of my apartment. I never see the other tenants, 'cept coming and going—and I like it that way and have a lot of privacy. Of course it does get a bit lonely at times, but I find that I'm more than willing to pay that price.

Thank you also for the delicious cake, Pam. It held up real well.

My weekly shopping consists of soap—tissues— coffee —sugar—toothpaste—and that's about it. What a change from the truckloads of previous years!

Had a ball with the girls. But, again, not enough time and I was too over-tired to really enjoy them. Would have liked to have given them more, but I couldn't. I've lost the capacity. Or I never had it but used to *think* I did. There is nothing—*nothing*—left in me to give. And this often feels like happiness.

Hope by now you've received my package and also that Ted's been definitely hired by Eastern. Regards to all.

Love,

Mom

"They do make a pair, don't they?"
"Well, I don't know, Teddy, it kind'v made me miss my Dad and my Mom already. . . ."
"Jesus, don't compare your folks to mine!"

"He's right, Pam," Rudi says from behind the newspaper. "*Your* Dad never tried to have *your* Mom put away."

Ted looks surprised, as if he didn't know Rudi knew that. Or as if he didn't know it himself.

"Your mother may be going the way of her sister, Grace," Rudi says. "After your Aunt Grace left the convent she vanished. And I think your mother is just gradually vanishing right now. You'll get a letter from her this winter or next spring and then you'll never hear from her again."

Pam and Ted exchange glances and Pam changes the subject.

"Hey wasn't my Dad something when he said that about taking the elevated line out to see the *tenements?*"

"He must've made a picture—as pale as he is and what's he up to now, about 270 pounds . . . !"

"People think they know who you are," Rudi says, sunlight falling on him in a way that makes him look like vividly tinted paper mâché. "Families think that they've hatched you and that their traits are your destiny. Two things are locked together, Pam. They're locked together like a pair of hands. And those two locked-together things are what we call Destiny. Do you know what those two things are, Pam?"

"No, I don't, Rudi. I don't know what they are and I don't know what you mean. But I sure don't think Mom and Dad think they *hatched* us. . . ."

"It is *possible* to escape from your destiny, Pam!"

"But why would anyone want to escape from his destiny, Rudi? What's wrong with our destiny?"

"People *assume* they have brothers and they *assume* those brothers come from California. But what if I'm *not* your brother and what if I *don't* come from California."

Rudi is on his feet, talking faster and faster. As far as Pam and Ted can make out he's saying pretty much the same thing, but in new and endless combinations, ten different ways, then fifty, then five hundred. It sounds like another language, or a sub-language, a code, like the crackling flash of particles when the tv loses its transmission. Ted rises to his feet also, his normally pink cheeks dead white, takes a step toward Rudi with nothing in particular in mind and stands there uselessly. Pam, trying to control herself, is sobbing in a wierd, smothered way.

The lamp cord is repaired and Ted is switching the lamp on and off with an expression of puzzled satisfaction. Pam is sitting where Rudi was sitting, leafing through the same out-dated *Sunday News.*

"I can't at all figure what set Rudi off," Ted says without looking at Pam.

"Dunno, Teddy," Pam says, a little distracted by a small article about a corpse that was found in their neighborhood a couple of days back, neck broken and ear lobes, several fingers and toes missing.

"Sometimes I think you're just about the only person on the face of the Earth he cares for. He has a very low opinion of people. I mean, I don't think he likes *anyone*."

"Yes, I think you're right. And I don't like it either. I don't like the fact that he tries to make someone so *pure* out of me. Because one day he's going to be sorely disappointed. If he looks at me as the last grain of hope for humanity and then I *fail* him. . . . It kind'v gets to be a burden when people keep telling you how *good* you are, Teddy."

"But you *are* good, Pammy."

Pam isn't listening. She's spotted an article that covers two facing pages with photographs on both. On the left-hand page there's a picture of an enormous man in a dark suit and narrow tie. He has a black wheatfield of hair flattened backward a bit, as if a tractor had just passed over it; eyebrows like drawbridges, one of them raised a little more than the other, letting those on the outside get a tiny glimpse of doubts or worries trying to gnaw their way out through the thick bone of the skull; an ordinary, perhaps smallish bulb nose, the nostrils maybe a drop wider than average; a slack mouth sucked in to look firm; eyes turned diagonally away from the camera or toward the edge of the page. The caption reads: "HEINZY HEINZ, THE PIED PIPER OF BENTON."

On the same page there's a photograph of two men: one, in white shirtsleeves and dark slacks, digging with a shovel in pale, ink-stained ground; the other, in a coarse-grained state trooper's uniform, leather holster and boots, moving off to the left down a shallow grade, his steps following his gaze into the underbrush. The caption reads: "Cop shovels desert sand in search of Jolene Gill, girl friend of killer, Adolph Heinz, the 'Benton Butcher,' whom she had found 'creepy' but 'nice.' "

On the facing page there's a row of three snapshots of women, one 4" x 3", two 3" x 2". The larger photograph shows a woman in a simple white blouse and dark skirt, left fist on left hip. Her dark hair is short yet windblown, windblown yet fixed in a permanent set of wig-like clusters, and her features are square-cut, pugilistic. She's looking out to the left, slightly down, toward a point far beyond the boundaries of the photograph or, perhaps, all possible vistas open to the photographer. The two smaller photos resemble high school yearbook photos of people you never knew or can't remember. The woman in the center photograph has a short hairdo with deep, rigid waves and dark blonde gleaming shadows. Neither pretty nor ugly, mouth wide open in a luckluster smile. Nose a tiny bulb. Dark eyes staring straight at the camera, straight *through* the camera, toward Pam or beyond her toward the next room, a room in a house in Benton, Arizona or beyond the planet's light envelope. The woman on the right-hand side of the page has a narrow face; weak chin; shoulder-length blonde hair, bobbed; eyes resting utterly within their own surface; mouth hammered in under the sum of ten cancelled expressions; forehead as short and fragile as the chin. The caption under the three photographs reads: "Mary English (left), drawn irresistably by the Pied Piper's pitch, stares down at the spot where once was heard a dying scream. Heinz's first of three victims, Jolene Gill (middle), and Gretchen Lenz, who vanished with her sister, Heidi."

Pam takes in the whole article swiftly, skimming each subsection under its boldface heading:

MEAN AND BEAUTIFUL

TALK TURNS TO MURDER

SHE HEARD A SCREAM

MOTHER TAILS 'HEINZY'

TAKES A BEATING

THREATENS TO TALK

OFF TO CALIFORNIA

SUGGESTS A BURIAL

A DUBIOUS STORY

LOSES HIS COOL

ESCAPE IN RED WIG

But Pam keeps returning to the photograph of Heinz. He looks exactly (with the solitary exception of the black, oddly flattened hair) like Rudi! Could just about be Rudi's double. She doesn't ever remember seeing two people look so much alike, not even Olivia de Havilland in the movie where she plays twin sisters. And she wonders: is it really possible that the man who's been living with them isn't Rudi? Could it be that in Las Vegas or maybe Reno, Tahoe or Gardena, or one of the places Rudi'd travelled to with Donald, possibly Galveston, Dallas, Norfolk or Newport News, or down across the border in Tijuana or up in Alaska, even in Libya or South Africa, this guy Heinz happened to run into Rudi? His exact duplicate. Not a second wasted in surprise. He saw what he had to do and did it. A fool-proof escape. It had to have happened during one of Rudi and Donald's arguments: they'd split up for the millionth time, hadn't rejoined. It really was possible! Rudi could be dead. This could be Heinz!

Ted is saying that he had a conversation with Donald about Rudi. He said: "I really wish Rudi could lose some weight, because he *is* a good-looking person." And Donald said: "Well, he *could* be a good-looking person, if only he'd lose some goddamn weight. I've been trying to get him onto that, Ted, believe me." So *he* said: "It does stand in his way, I think—in the way of having any normal sort of social life." "Yes," Donald said, "it sure as hell is some sort of obstacle. There aren't too many women who're going to be interested in a two-tonner!"

177

"If it were only just his weight!" Pam hears herself cry out.

Ted begins to read the shopping list from a pink slip of paper, but leaves off in the middle.

"Why is it that grocery shopping always gets me down?" he says.

He doesn't say that it has less to do with grocery shopping than with the darkening light over the roofs and less to do with the darkening light over the roofs than with something he's never been able and never will be able to name.

"No," Ted says, dejected, "it isn't just the weight."

A man is walking, searching for something he'll recognize only when he's found it. He passes through a zone of run-down storefronts, railroad flats, bars and shanties—all those unhappy surfaces that have put down such deep roots into reality. Hours later he passes through a residential zone with its pseudo-chateaux ringed round with layered depths of park-like lawn and hemlock screen. Toward dusk he crosses a scorched green plaza receding toward a pale sky over water and the blue oxidized green of a bridge. As he makes his way toward the ocean he thinks: one's gaze withers in the terrible gaze of the world. And one's soul, exactly like the great balloon of one's shadow, searches for a deeper shadow to hide in.

The moon is full, its enormous, dully glowing face like a face in a highrise window. Currents stream by it. Micro-particles that taken together may = life pass into warm breezes on Earth's beaches, prickling the hair on the heads and forearms of strolling couples. Someone fishing reels up a bright little angle of light. A tiny, dark figure dashes into bright waves; a pale figure into dark waves.

A match flares up, a tiny fire below the horizon.

A little moisture seeps out of the white matchstick paper below the head.

An enormous man is lighting a cigarette from a pack he doesn't remember buying.

One puff to make sure the tobacco has taken the flame.

He can feel, through his fingertips, that something is boring into itself, away from the dark cone of ash, toward his lips and mouth. It wants to get inside him, where it can tunnel toward the dark green lake of the trees along the avenues; beyond the avenues; beyond the long meadows and miniature evergreen forests of the national park; toward a black, orbiting zone that knows nothing of the pleasant surface of things, of friendship or happiness.

The dark, evergreen lights of a ship on the horizon seem to him the green of a green glass ashtray with a round bowl and notches at the four corners, a beautiful leaf green that casts green facets on the polished wood of a table. He wonders if it's possible to reach out and stamp his cigarette out in it.

Someone lights a cigarette not twenty feet away. A woman's blonde curls show up in the flare of the match: fiftyish with a pug nose, short bulldog jaw. He feels drawn to her, as if she were pulling at his flame through her cigarette. He feels his hips and shoulders, arms and ankles twine with hers, faces close and talking, sharing the cigarette of happiness rather than the far more popular cigarette of unhappiness. His shadow flies toward her and is completely surprised to find that it can't get through. It smashes up against her, quivers and sticks there, like a dart in a dartboard.

As if the sound of someone pounding in a nail can be heard in a room seven blocks away.

Or as if the phone is ringing and someone is desperately trying to get in touch.

You wake up, feeling parted forever from a world of the utmost intimacy, from an urgency of feeling you never know in waking life—an unspeakable depth of anguish, of humiliation or love. As if, having actually succeeded in travelling beyond death, your arms around a loved one, a blue crystal drifting swiftly among crystals, along a dark, curved track beyond the barrier of all inward-travelling forces, something draws it all away as easily as the cotton sheet that covers you in summer, exposing you to ordinary morning light.

Ted remembers dreaming that the telephone gave one short burst and that he found himself standing in his bathrobe, holding the receiver before the noise had travelled beyond the fringe of the red oval rug. Now he's awake and holding the receiver. Someone at the other end is talking so rapidly, in arpeggios, that he reaches the other end of his keyboard and begins to flurry backward. Ted's voice is nothing but glue. The two men talk for several minutes without understanding a word.

After a while the man at the other end gets his voice straightened out and Ted realizes it's Rudi. Rudi says that he just woke up in this hotel and both his arms are numb. He thinks that he fell asleep and dreamed that he was dreaming. In one of those dreamed dreams he turned over and slept on his hands. He *never* sleeps on his hands. What happened last night to make him sleep on his hands!

He goes off into another row of arpeggios and Ted tells him not to move till he gets there.

The door of the hotel is the burglar-resistant kind, with a wire lattice embedded in the glass and a heavy steel frame. The stairs leading to the upper stories are covered with a brilliant runner of vermillion and orange diamonds. At the first landing there's an alcove, but no desk clerk, no desk with numbered pigeon-holes and keys or any other interior map or blueprint. A red-and-black bookkeeper's ledger is lying open on an old, green felt-surfaced card table. Ted leafs through it: nothing but figures that might be the hotel's accounts, a gambler's private code or rough computations for building a flying saucer like the one sighted in summer of 1983 over the police station in Carmel, New York.

He sets off down the narrow corridor, tapping at one door, then another. A rather deep woman's voice answers from the first. No one answers from the second. The third door (the three doors are so close together they form a cluster) is wide open. The room seems unoccupied: a stained and pitted green-brown-light green-cocoa-striped mattress mounted on a dark set of springs on short, bowed legs; a wash basin; white kitchen chair. The machinery of this region is so powerful and efficient, a gas-less engine of misery powered by the fall-out of absolutely everything, that a glance into it makes Ted feel suddenly downcast, hopeless. The carpet is a dark, dry stain that runs from one end of things to the other. The grey walls may once have been the pleasant, pale blue of blue clouds that are more like blue markings in a blue sky than discrete objects. "Life really has only one principle," Ted thinks unhappily. "Or it has a lot of principles, but they all run down the same drain. . . ." He's arrived at another sequence of doors. Three on the left, two on the right. Voices are coming from somewhere within this constellation. He hears a little water running in a sink, a woman's voice, hoarse from cigarette smoking, a man's voice, somewhere between Rudi's timbre and shading and Laird Cregar's in *I Wake Up Screaming.*

The man says something like "I'm trying to think about my mother."

"What for?"

"Because I can't remember her. It wasn't that long ago—but all I can see is a woman with a blonde wig."

"Is that all?"

"She's about your height."

"No kidding. . . ."

"Really!"

A little low laughter.

"Do you have many friends?"

"No."

"Nobody?"

"I have a friend, Edward."

"Yes. . . ?"

"Yes. When I'm with Edward . . . then everything's alright. I feel ok. With Edward everything's ok. There's something about Edward that makes me feel good."

"What is it about Edward that makes you feel good?"

"I don't know."

"What's he like?"

"There's something about him."

"But you can't put your finger on it."

"How did you know? That's it. I never though of it, but it's true. There's something about him, something that's *not like me.* It makes me feel ok, but I can't put my finger on it. . . ."

"Would you like to be like Edward?"

"Like Edward?"

"You admire him. Edward is sure of himself. He's smooth with people. He has fun. And you'd like to be that way too. Is that it?"

"No, that's not it," the man says, his voice altering in an ambiguous but important way. "Edward is as bad as I am. And he's stupider. So I don't think I want to be like him. We're *all* ill. Do I mean 'ill'? All our faculties are asleep. We talk about 'health' the way we talk about life on another planet. Do you understand what I'm saying?"

"No, honey, I don't."

"Good. There are things I don't want anybody to understand. I want to talk about them, but I don't want anybody to understand them. There are things. . . ."

"There are things you didn't tell those stupid detectives. I knew it!"

"You know me, Rita. Better than anyone does."

"But I hardly know you at all . . . !"

"Am I the type who takes walks? Do I stroll on the boardwalk on a summer evening? Do I go down to the shore to stare at sunsets?"

"God forbid!" the woman laughs.

"But I remember *being* there. I remember *doing* those things."

"Sometimes a feeling is so strong you think it's a memory. Like a dream you've had so often. . . ."

The man says that on the boardwalk or on the beach at night, not long after sunset, when you're still able to feel darkness as something tangible, as something odd, an extraordinary state, the ordinary human mortal is amazed by the number of lights passing through the air. Some of them are ships, floating in the opening that's visible between two horizons. But the roaring and trembling overhead remind him that he's close to a major airport. Planes take off and approach every couple of minutes, or even less. He sees them pass overhead at different heights and angles—looking very distant and abstract—the usual arrays of red and green lights—or low and menacing, dark as submarines. Some of the lights hovering over the ocean, yellow and round— larger, more globe-like and orange the longer they hover—are simply planes in holding patterns. Sometimes there's a small light, red or deep blue, flattened and twinkling, that moves in a swift, erratic way. Some of these lights seem to vanish backward or upward; they zip away without reappearing somewhere along the loop of a turn.

After the normal human mortal has stood there for a while, watching things appear and depart, he's pierced by an odd sort of unhappiness. He thinks: this is the modern sky. He really is witnessing the appearance of the modern world. This is actually the way it looks when it looks modern but isn't *trying* to look modern. And he knows for certain how limited, how trapped he is— exactly like people in another century who weren't able to get far beyond their valley, with its handful of dull but pretty towns.

Before long there'll be a completely different modern sky. But you won't see it. That much is certain. You long to see an object—what we call "an unidentified flying object"—something that sails right through the limits of the modern sky. You feel that you can't live another second in the normal way. The only thing that can cure you is to get on a rocket, travel twenty-five light years to a region where the idea of the future doesn't resemble Fort Worth. But nothing appears. You don't travel to another planet and the feeling passes off. If not one other thing is learned in life, every idiot seems to learn this: that there's no event, no matter how much dread it causes beforehand or how much anguish afterward, that doesn't fade into the rest. The disappearance of events, emotions and memories is so regular and predictable, so precise, we ought to be able to work out a formula for it. The familiar feeling of "letdown" is the body's feeble yearning to remember. Exactly what's supposed to console us, is what makes life terrible. . . .

"Jesus, honey, whad'ya mean by 'an ordinary human mortal'? You make it sound like there's something else."

"In Manhattan right now, Rita, the atmosphere is the color of aluminum. You wouldn't be surprised to see waves breaking against the middle levels of the high-rises. There's a woman in a white high-rise standing at her picture window, where there's an almost level glimpse of the river, thinking that the visible moat of space that usually separates us from things looks filled in. You couldn't slip one hand between the outer skin of the building and the world beyond. The air has the weight of sea water. It reminds her of the week she spent in Puerto Rico, when there was a shark attack at a resort further along the coast and people just stood on the beach, afraid to go in—the sky and the water such a horrible, tinny color you not only sensed them cruising and waiting out there, but you knew that their world lay so flat against yours that one of them might slide right up to you, at eye level, and grab you right off the beach. . . ."

"Would you like to go down now and get some breakfast . . . ?"

"There's something else. . . ."

"Won't it keep?"

"I have the feeling I've done something horrible, unforgivable. They're going to punish me for it! The punishment was ready and waiting before I did it . . . !"

"You can hide. I can hide you. There's this place up near the Connecticut-New York-Massachusetts border on the way to Mt. Washington, you can't really call it a hotel. . . ."

"There used to be a way of getting out. But I've forgotten it. It used to be my own language, but now it's foreign. You choose something and then you're trapped in it. . . ."

"We can talk about it in the diner, baby. It'll be better down there with the fake flowers and the brass sconces. Nobody goes wierd in the diner."

"I love when you call me baby."

"Baby, baby. . . ."

A little throaty laughter.

"You know, you're a lot like Edward."

"Me? I'm like Edward . . . ?"

Very loud sound of chairs moving.

Ted hurries back down the corridor and out of the hotel as silently and quickly as he can.

He crosses the street and conceals himself in the shallow doorway of the real estate office between the bakery and the discount store.

He waits ten minutes or more, but no one comes out.

He isn't at all sure if it was Rudi. Isn't sure it *wasn't* Rudi either. The guy talked about "Edward." "Ted" is a diminutive of

"Edward." But no one has ever called Ted Edward. Also: if it were Rudi, he'd be talking about Donald Green. Rudi and Donald: that would be possible. Ted has had thoughts about *those* two. But for Rudi to talk that way about him would mean that Rudi had become close to him in some wierd way without his knowing it! That for Rudi he was another Ted. And if he *was* another Ted for Rudi, then Rudi might have named that Ted "Edward."

Ted doesn't know what to do. He could go back in, go back up, and knock at that door. Settle things swiftly, directly. Like turning, after fleeing through corridors, mounting stairways, hiding in cellars, to confront the madman who's stalking you with a Chinese cleaver. But knocking at that door is just one thing he can't face. He feels that it would be more possible to stand in the doorway of the real estate office all day, as immobile as someone who's had a stroke, wheeled this way and that under a golf cap, unable to turn your head, than to go back in and knock at that door.

What he'd really like to do is find a telephone, call Pam and ask *her* what to do. "Should I go back to the hotel? Go home? Look for Rudi in all the groceries and luncheonettes? Or what?"

But he can't do that either. If he calls Pam he has to tell her that her brother's out here, wandering around somewhere or sitting in a room on the second floor of a hotel, completely lost and thinking he's someone else.

The squat angles of an enormous pair of dusky blue trousers appear through the heavy burglar-proof door of the hotel, filling up its wire diamonds and blotting out the orange and vermillion runner.

The man stops on the pavement to clean his glasses. The world looks like a tremendous glass doorknob. Even with his glasses back in place, every direction looks like a facet of every other direction; every destination as far away as the enormous bank of early morning clouds that hasn't yet been drawn off below the horizon. Might as well set off toward those dark mountains as toward anywhere else.

Familiar dark range of mountains where once there may have

been an ocean, its blues and blacks darker and more tarnished than the hulls of freighters.

Familiar ocean where there once were mountains and will be mountains again.

The low, uneven line of the roofs above the dismal shop windows, the pizza joints and luncheonettes. The sidewalk with its grey, permanent stains and sour black puddles below the curb. The world is sailing through this dreary station without making a stop.

Minutes later the bottom of outer space begins to sift particles dryer than rain and moister than smoke on everything in sight.

Ted props himself up in bed. He smells coffee perking, the complex aromas of singed toast and browned butter. Rudi is snoring behind the wall, asleep and dreaming in the blue nursery, sending off the usual thermal, bioelectric and chemical outlines, like a wide-screen color television someone's forgotten to turn off.

He hears sobbing in the living room or kitchen, stumbles to the door in his dark bathrobe. Pam is sitting in a chair by the dinette table whose roundness forces a round sense of space on the zone by the kitchen, her head so far down it looks like she's throwing up. The radio is on, tuned to a twenty-four-hour station.

Pam says that a report just came over the radio that the body of Marian Lamb, the downstairs tenant, was washed up last night off the Point, her neck broken, her ear lobes and several fingers and toes missing, just like that other poor man they'd found near here a few weeks ago.

She looks up and meets Ted's glance.

"Don't say it!" she screams. "It isn't true! It *can't* be true! I won't listen to it!"

"But I'm not saying anything, honey," he murmurs.

Ted's little sister, Betty, is sitting between Ted and Rudi on the red couch. They're all watching a situation comedy on television. Betty is laughing, Ted is half-smiling and Rudi is reading *TV Guide* as if it were *Scientific American.*

Rudi says that there's a Lionel Atwill film already on on another channel. He cantilevers forward to turn the dial.

Betty, pouting, wants to know who "Lionel Atwill" is.

"You've seen him a million times, Betty," Rudi says. "But you don't know him. He's *invisible* to you. Everything is invisible to you. Is it because you only see what you want to see? I don't think so. I don't think you even see what you *want* to see. And you don't see what's there to see either. You don't see the surface and you don't see what's hidden. So what *do* you see, Betty? You're still not *completely* stupid because you're young. But it gets worse as you get older. Your brain gets smaller and smaller. By the time you're your brother's age it'll be the size of an orange pit."

Betty has tears in her eyes. But Ted doesn't intervene.

Rudi turns toward the television, sitting on the edge of the couch as if he can't get close enough to the screen.

Lionel Atwill is standing next to a corpse covered with a sheet and saying: "This is death by strangulation, gentle-men. And strangulation by an *unusually* powerful set of hands. Note the deep impression of the *thumb* marks on the *throat*. . . ." Someone else, a policeman or a reporter, says: "But what about this deep incision at the base of the brain, doctor?" "Yes," Atwill answers, "undoubtably inflicted by a surgical scal-pel."

A little later Atwill is explaining the possible character type of the killer: "Undoubtedly a neurotic. Someone with a deep pattern of activity held in a *knot*—a sort of knot in the *brain*. And anything can trigger off the need to commit this act *again* and *again*. To return to the original moment. *Anything*. The full moon—the sound of the ocean—and so on." "But why this *incision*, doctor?" "That is not merely an *incision*. This is clearly a case of *cannibalism*, gentle-men."

Later there's a headline that says SCRUBWOMAN IS MOON KILLER'S LATEST VICTIM. The police are convinced that the murderer is a member of the Academy. Atwill begs them to give him one last chance to clear the mystery up himself. He gathers all the Academy members in his laboratory in Cliff Manor on Blackstone Shoals, Long Island, administers a sort of lie detector test. Everyone (including Atwill himself) is strapped into a chair fitted out with dozens of meters, coils, electronic monitors. The camera pans across the row of strapped-in doctors. Dr. Wells, who did the treatise on cannibalism and who's missing one hand. Old Dr. Haines, the one who's kept a heart alive electrically for months and who secretly reads a magazine called *French Thrills*. And the two doctors (one in a wheelchair, one with something odd about his hands) who survived the shipwreck and the days of starvation in the lifeboat, while their companions perished or disappeared. When all the equipment is glowing and buzzing Atwill says: "Naturally I would prefer to believe that all members of the Academy are *innocent*. But, unfortunately, circumstances—the use of a surgical scal-pel used *only* by this institution, for example—prove that *one* of us may be *guilty*. *Any* one of us. Someone in this room may be a murderer. A man who *kills* by the light of a full moon with a surgical *in-stru-ment*. And who leaves his victims horribly *mutilated*. It is my *theory* that the murderer is someone who through *dire necessity* was compelled to resort to cannibalism. And that instant was *hammered into his brain* like a *nail*. Clever and brilliant, he is able to *conceal* his thoughts from his colleagues. *But not from this radiograph*." The radiograph switch is thrown, the laboratory goes black, spasms of light pulse in panels and coils, someone screams as if stabbed, everyone cries out, struggles against the thongs binding him into his chair. The scene shifts to another room. Someone with one hand like an animal's claw is smearing bogs of greyish, flesh-like jelly on his face and muttering, "SYNTHETIC FLESH! SYNTHETIC FLESH!"

Betty screams.

"SYNTHETIC FLESH!" Rudi screams, his voice perfectly synchronized with the madman's. "Exactly the same as raw living flesh eaten by cannibals! SYNTHETIC FLESH!"

Betty dashes to the door and Rudi follows her. Ted continues to watch television.

The old brass floor lamp with its enormous shade casts a broad circle of light on the floor-boards surrounding the red oval rug. The disc of silence that surrounds it within a vast perimeter of tiny sounds is disturbing.

Ted picks up the double highball glass that's gleaming, half clear, half amber, on the coffee table, drains half of its contents, and sits shivering in the big armchair.

By the time he sets the wide glass with its extra bottom weight down on the table's glass surface, Ted is empty and exhausted while the glass is 1/8 full of dark amber thoughts.

"No refuge—no sanctuary. Is it true that without love there's no sanctuary on earth—nothing . . . ? Totally alone and adrift—

"A corpse is already in you. Traveling with you. Always horizontal—

"So that when you lie down there's a fatal harmony—

"All your life you feel this anxiety—this tug of the horizontal—

"At night you leap up so suddenly your weight can still be felt on the bed—more or less at the moment two hands of the clock are about to coincide—

"You died *before* you were alive—

"Slowly life struggles to assert itself—

"Dies out before a good blaze can get started—"

Ted is draining the surprisingly heavy glass of its last thoughts when Betty bursts into the room screaming his name and crying.

"What is it, honey?" Ted says without moving.

It looks as if she's about to fall on him, he realizes she wants to be embraced and embraces her.

"It's Rudi! It's Rudi! Oh Ted! It's *Rudi!*"

"Rudi?" he says dumbly.

Betty has him clasped close and is sobbing into his shirt.

"You didn' *see* him! You didn' see what he *looked* like . . . ! DON'T LET HIM IN! DON'T LET HIM IN! HE'S COMING . . . !"

Only her throat is holding her voice together. It's a quiver of trills.

"Hey, it's only good old Rudi, Betty. It's only *make*-believe."

Betty, letting go, is looking aghast at the door.

Ted actually thinks he hears a board creak in the hall, but tells Betty that he doesn't hear a thing.

He strokes Betty's hair indifferently and Betty gradually calms down.

Time is passing in any number of ways. The television, switched off (or, rather, *not* switched on) seems to have a perpetual, fluid calendar of instants locked inside. So that it's possible to think: if no one ever watches television again, Time will be cancelled. The room is almost dark. The floor lamp is switched off and the small table lamp emits a glow more like a candle than anything else. A level, simultaneous plane of time extends endlessly from this weak oval.

Ted is sitting over in one corner of the long red couch, doing nothing, near dozing, like someone staring into the fire. Betty is taking up the rest of the couch with her long, smooth legs, dark blue shorts of soft cotton, pale blue polo, slender arms holding a *National Geographic*.

A while later Betty has turned over onto her stomach. She's asleep, her left hand and the yellow cover of the magazine within the weak oval of light intersecting with the red oval of the rug. Ted falls asleep and dreams that he's having a fight with Pam. He goes up to his room (in the dream he lives in a house with two or three stories, just as he did in childhood). He tries one lamp, then another, all the while longing to sit quietly in the dark, to be like a monk who's taken a vow of darkness. The lamps blink on and off several times and then go dead, as if he's willed it. A woman comes in, calling out a name that he recognizes, though it isn't his name or the name of anyone he knows. It's the name of *something*. What is that something? He can't name it.

At first the woman sees no one, though she's left the door open and a sort of twilight washes through the heavier particles of darkness. She catches sight of him sitting there, barely visible within a high-backed chair, and she's frightened. They both turn in terror. The murderer's come through the door. His hair stands out against the light.

Ted wakes up, his heart racing. There isn't a sound in the apartment, perhaps not in the house. It's so silent that Betty's sleeping isn't enough to cause it. Rudi must be sleeping too. Voices in the street, down on the sidewalk, are like the voices you make out on shore when you're about to row out of sight. He crosses to the window, leans out to see if it's Pam. His face and yellow/brown curls are tinted the same wierd amber-coral that's tinting the yellow stucco walls of the three-tier hacienda-style house diagonally across the way. But it isn't Pam. It's the tall musician who lives next door and his tall musician friend, who's married to the musician's sister, attaching a U-Haul trailer to his old Buick.

The rest of the night is spent worrying about Pam, dozing, imagining he hears Pam arriving, looking at the tv or out the window.

About one a.m. people are actually coming up the stairs. Now that they *are* arriving, he can tell that a real arrival sounds different in every way from all those false alarms. A real arrival has an unmistakable texture and weight. It has definite early signals and then gathers force and mass. It doesn't begin with a murmur of neutral voices you don't quite recognize and the rattle of a heavy chain against a fender. It *does* begin with a front door closing, laughter you'd recognize after five deaths and six lifetimes, overlapping heavy treads on carpeted stairs, an enveloping breath of the out-of-doors you can feel welling up from a distance.

Pam comes in with Donald. Her eyes are glowing, cheeks flushed. Ted feels an idiotic yearning, as if they've just met. He thinks to himself that Pam hasn't looked this good since before they were married, when she had a high-level job with Hydra Chemical.

"Where's Frankenstein?" Donald asks.

"Asleep, most likely," Ted says tonelessly. He's so taken by the way Pam looks that he's depressed by it.

Pam says that Rudi *can't* be sleeping, cause she looked into his room on the way in and he wasn't there. Bed was still made.

Ted says that Rudi *did* pull some pretty wierd stunts tonight. Scared poor Betty half out of her skull.

"What *kind'v* wierd stunts, Teddy?"

"Pretty wierd, that's all."

There's an odd silence, one with a furry edge, like a torn blotter.

Ted starts to say: "I didn't know you guys were going out together tonight," but Pam interrupts him.

"Donny's leaving for Alaska tonight. And I'm going with him."

Ted says that he has to drive Betty home.

"Jesus, Ted," Donald says. "I feel lousy as hell about this. I didn't wanna come up here at all. But, if you'll stop and think about it, Pam and I go back *way* before. . . ."

Ted is already carrying little Betty down the stairs.

Donald follows Ted to the head of the stairs.

"Be a little *honest* with yourself, Ted!" he yells down the stairwell, though Ted may already be out the front door. "You're a fuckn *seed* pod, Ted! You belong with *Rudi,* Ted!"

Several weeks later, in a street in the same neighborhood or one exactly like it, an unusually thin woman is standing in front of her house, in warm sunlight, hosing down her black Newfoundland. Her younger daughter Rosamond is watching how the spray carries over to the spruce next door. The young needles are green and shining while the rest of the tree looks as if it has a web over it and inside, under the boughs, it's as black as a cave.

An enormous man who's passing, in clothing that's stained green and brown, as if he's been sleeping on lawns, under hedges, or in back gardens or in a park somewhere, stops and says: "A pine *tree* is exactly like a pine *cone.* But what is a pine *cone* exactly like?"

The woman has the dog soaked and mother and daughter begin to scrub him into a lather.

"You have a second self," the man continues, "and you feel it slipping away. Tears of jealousy come to your eyes when you see your ex-husband's face on the cover of *TV Guide.*"

He's examining her closely, as if this sign or that will make him do one thing or another.

"I've been watching you and your children. I've been watching your children grow. I've seen everything that's happened. And I just want to tell you that I don't like your daughter, Johanna!"

"Johanna?" the woman answers stupidly. She's panic-stricken because the man knows her elder daughter's name.

"I don't like her dreams. When she wakes up screaming in the middle of the night and you can't quiet her down, when she sobs uncontrollably, for one hour or two, I know she's dreaming of me. And I don't like it!"

The younger daughter, Rosamond, is crying and pulling at her mother's slacks. The mother's gone dead white, her arm around her daughter. The black Newfoundland is barking and dripping soap suds, taking nervous steps forward and back. It gathers its courage, finds leverage, bounds, accelerates, detonates into the man's chest, jaws swivelled toward the throat. The man staggers and bends under the impact, his eyes and the dog's eyes no more than a foot apart. His arms are deep in fur, as if it were a sinkful of water. The forearms are covered with slobber and blood. The dog's choked snarls turn into screams. Something pops in the structure of the dog's thick neck and its body drops to the rounded slope of the lawn, not quite in the long shadow of a neighbor's spruce.

The man's enormous stained white shirt and dark slacks fly into the gap between two houses before the woman is able to utter a sound.

Ted's little sister, Betty, is at home, in her room, lying on her bed, unable to do her homework. Her head is a leather helmet of stupidity that will eventually become a familiar and comfortable as a regular head. She observes that the shiny red material of the bedspread has here and there, regularly or randomly, a coarse, raised thread in it. She gets tired of lying there and figuring out the bedspread as if it were a problem in solid geometry, goes to her vanity and begins brushing her short curls with harsh strokes. Her scalp burns as if it were about to bleed.

She turns. Someone is outside her door, breathing, listening. A board creaks slowly, as if weight is being gradually released, shifted from one leg to the other. The sensation continues then dissipates. There are no sounds in the hall or on the stairs and no door can be heard opening or closing.

Betty goes to the window. Her glance flies without hesitation toward a point in the distance, where it seems to her she sees Rudi, standing, as if waiting for a bus, under the trees at the intersection.

Below the porches of nine frame houses, a powerful wind is blowing through evergreen shrubs. Someone standing in the triple shadow of a fir or hemlock (precisely the height of the three-tier house it measures) imagines he's standing in an evergreen forest, a sort of black thistle. A whole mountain, a massive cone of wooded slopes, revolves through the universe at 360° per second. He thinks to himself: from the slopes the monster descends on mountain hamlets—children vanish, bodies are dismembered, local crackpots falsely convicted of murder. Down through the ages men have become beasts: the snarling and drooling of nightmares a nocturnal way of life.

Ted hasn't gone to work for weeks. He hasn't gone grocery shopping, hasn't left the apartment, hasn't shaved or bathed. He's been watching television eighteen hours a day and eating whatever food was in the refrigerator when Pam left and everything that can be eaten straight from the can or heated. It's 11 p.m. and he's eating from a tin of Campbell's Barbecue Style Pork & Beans while he watches the news gliding up against the inner surface of the screen. The story comes over of the capture in northwestern Connecticut of an escaped murderer, the famous "Benton Butcher." The man's already confessed to the murders, either alone or with the participation of a man he refuses to name, of two hundred women and children in states along the Northeastern Seaboard, in the Southwest and in the Far West.

A quick glimpse of a tremendous man with red hair being hurried up the steps of a courthouse.

The red hair is obviously a disguise: a hasty dye job or even a wig.

Ted goes to the phone, gets the number of the police in the town named in the news report and calls.

"The guy you pulled in," he says, "the big guy with the red hair who confessed to all those murders, is *not* the one you think he is! He is *not* some guy from Arizona! This guy you've got up there is my brother-in-law who disappeared three weeks ago! He's just a dead ringer for the other guy, that's all. Who am *I*? Whad'ya mean who am I? What difference does it make who *I* am?"

He lowers the receiver from his ear, stares at it without replacing it in the cradle. He looks out the window, straight ahead over the tiled or shingled, flat or peaked roofs, then to the left, toward the ocean. The sky is unusually light and the atmosphere is perfectly clear and calm. Nothing is closed. Every window is open. He feels that he can see through the pale row of apartment buildings, all the way to the west, where the full length of the New Jersey coast is visible. A dark, unstable blue, an internally burning cobalt, impossible to remember five seconds after you look away. It breaks down instantly into more luminous ideas of blue, darker memories.

One light grows larger and more brilliant as the atmosphere darkens. Smaller and dimmer lights appear far to the right, near the point where the dark blue line of the Jersey coast and the pale, curved line of New York's sand beaches converge. Here and there, to the left, one sees a small cluster above the horizon, rising and dipping as if afloat on the water.

Everything helps darkness arrive.

A hand is stroking a child's head, slipping in between its sobs and delivering it to a calm and friendly world

Or a hand does *not* slip in, does *not* stroke the child's head— the infant simply lies there, exhausted from sobbing, feeling delivered to a world of dark rooms and windows.

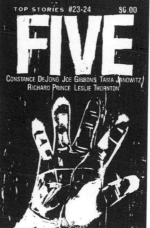

TOP STORIES #23-24 $6.00

FIVE

CONSTANCE DEJONG JOE GIBBONS TAMA JANOWITZ
RICHARD PRINCE LESLIE THORNTON

JOKES

BY RICHARD PRINCE

"My Doctor sure put me back on my feet."
"Really?"
"Yeah, when I got his bill, I hadda sell my car!"

"Which reminds me of the doctor who knew his patient couldn't afford an operation, so he 'retouched' his X-rays."

"My mother and father keep fighting. They rant and they rave and they shout."
"Who is your father?" somebody asked.
"That's what they're fighting about."

A traveling salesman stopped by a farmhouse and asked for a night's lodging.

"We're all filled up," said the farmer, "but you can sleep with the little redheaded schoolteacher."

"That's alright," said the traveling salesman, "I'm a perfect gentleman."

"Fine," said the farmer, "so is the little redheaded school-teacher!"

I gave her so many gifts I had to marry her for my money.

Fireman pulling drunk out of a burning bed: You darned fool, that'll teach you to smoke in bed.
Drunk: I wasn't smoking in bed, it was on fire when I laid down.

Camp Hiawatha, that's where the Jewish kids go for the summer. Camp Ginsberg, that's where the Indian kids go for the summer.

A couple is driving to Miami Beach in a brand new car. As they're driving he puts his hand on her knee. She says, "We're married now, you can go a little farther." So he went to Fort Lauderdale.

Jewish man talking to his friend: If I live I'll see you Tuesday. If I don't I'll see you Wednesday.

"I eat politics and I sleep politics, but I never *drink* politics."

TOURIST ATTRACTIONS

TOP STORIES #25-26 $6.00

TOURIST ATTRACTIONS

DOUGLAS BLAU•LINDA L. CATHCART
CHERYL CLARKE•SUSAN DAITCH
CONSTANCE DEJONG•ROBERT FIENGO
GARY INDIANA•SUZANNE JACKSON
•CARYL JONES-SYLVESTER•
JUDY LINN•MICKI MCGEE
GLENN O'BRIEN•SEKOU SUNDIATA
LYNNE TILLMAN•JANE WARRICK

GRAN TURISMO

BY GLENN O'BRIEN

Last year in Biarritz I met this biker chick at the Casino. She was tall, blonde, Finnish. We both won big on the don't pass line and without a real word between us we got out of there. She had a Vincent Black Shadow with a side car parked in front. I had my Gran Turismo in the lot but she said she needed someone to balance out the bike going down the mountain.

I hopped in and we gunned off into the hot night. Her leathers were the color of the full moon. I leaned out of the sidecar on the turns. She took them fast. She headed for the French border.

Before we got to the checkpoint she stopped at the side of the road, handed me a wallet and took off again. We passed the border without incident. We had passed from Spain to France but we were still in Basque country.

She stopped again at the side of the road, this time to open a gate in a wire fence that enclosed a wooded hillside. We climbed the hill and at the top was a cement chateau with a tower. She lived there with Arturo, her brother, a stylist, and his Brazilian girlfriend YeYe.

YeYe was swimming naked in the pool and Arturo was riding a

stationary bicycle when we arrived. He told us to help ourselves to champagne and we did.

Then Ikipope the butler arrived and asked us if we had eaten. In a few minutes he returned with piping bowls of Mulligitawny soup and some bread.

The biker chick, Helena, looked nothing like her brother, but she explained that her mother had been a stewardess for Pan Am. Her father was a pilot from Lufthansa and Arturo's father was a Brazilian copra baron with a spurious title.

Arturo had attended hotel management school at Cornell where he played reserve point guard on the basketball team, but after graduation he had attended beauty school, followed by a brief stint as a minor league pro in the Continental Basketball Association. Returning to Paris he had been discovered by Vogue and he'd been in the money ever since, working as a stylist for the top photographers in the business.

He traveled all over the world, and on one shoot in Bali he had met YeYe who was working as a dancercize instructor and helped choreograph the Robert Palmer rock video Arturo was working on with Guy Bourdin. YeYe was only half Balinese, her father was an actor who had visited the island during the filming of South Pacific. They had been together ever since.

Helena was harder to figure. She was young. She said she went to school but she wouldn't say more. She changed into a white one-piece bathing suit and put on a tape of Slim Harpo. While she danced to "Hip Shake," I did the original rhythm part with spoons on the formica bar top.

Later we went out and looked at the cactuses in the moonlight. They seemed to have weird human and insect shapes. We talked about Paul Bowles, Ernest Hemingway and jai alai. Her cousin Nicky played jai alai in Newport, Rhode Island. We talked about Klaus von Bulow and picking rosehips on the beachwalk in Newport.

We heard a single engine plane circling above us but we saw no lights.

When we returned to the chateau Arturo and YeYe had gone to bed. Helena took out a large photo album and we sat on the floor looking through it and drinking port. Helena showed me her pictures of Reinnes Le Chateau where she said the Knights Templar had their headquarters and hid their treasure. She told me a long story having something to do with Victor Hugo and Jean Cocteau being direct descendants of Jesus Christ and Grandmaster of the Elders of Zion. Then she asked me if she could wash my feet with her hair. It sounded pretty kinky to me, so I said, "Why not?"

She unrolled her bun and it reached practically to the floor. I couldn't believe it. I'd never seen hair that long in my life. I asked if I could wash my feet first before she washed them and she said that would ruin it, so I just sat back and let the girl do her thing.

After she washed my feet with her hair they were really clean. I asked her if she wanted to keep washing and she did. It was the best cleaning job I ever had.

I stayed up there with Helena and Arturo and YeYe for a few days and then Helena said she had to go away so I went back to Biarritz and got my car and drove all night to Paris and didn't see a cop all the way.

I checked into the Georges Cinq and went out to get a hamburger. I picked up a Herald Tribune and saw that the Yankees had beat the Red Sox 6 to 5. I thought of Helena and I wondered if her cousin Nicky, the jai alai player in Newport, was a Red Sox fan. When I returned to the hotel I opened my old, beat up Louis Vuitton overnighter and discovered I had someone else's bag. Beat up just like mine. But its contents were a lot different. Silk, nylon, pearls. I looked for a name. But all I found was an ounce of heroin.

I went to the Cafe Flor and had six gin and tonics before I knew what to do. I returned to the hotel, ordered a sandwich in aluminum foil from roomservice, made a small line of the drug on the foil and smoked it. Then I ate half the sandwich and went to the bathroom and threw up. When I emerged from the bathroom there was a pounding at the door. Woozy, it seemed to be the beating of my heart. I felt myself sinking into the shag carpet as I wavered toward the throbbing door. I threw open the door and a Chinese women dressed in black whisked past me into the room. I latched the door. She sniffed the air.

"I hope I'm not interrupting," she said.

"Not at all," I said. "Have we met?"

Her name was Lucille O'Malley. Her mother was from a wealthy Hong Kong banking family, her father was an Indy car driver who crashed and burned in the seventies. She was the ideal of Chinese beauty, but with pale blue eyes.

"I am a friend of Helena," she said.

I wondered if my feet were clean.

"She said that she left something with you on the road from Biarritz and needs it back."

I remembered Helena passing me the wallet just before we had crossed the border into France. I remembered the strange look of those cactuses in her backyard.

Later that night at a night club Lucille gave me a big hickey on my neck and introduced me to a lot of her friends and we went back to her house and listened to Zulu records and chased the dragon some more. An American saxophone player came over and we played a few rubbers of bridge.

I woke up in Lucille's bed. She was out. She came back with the Herald Tribune and coffee. The Red Sox beat the Tigers 2 zip—Oil Can Boyd had a two hitter going in the seventh when he was ejected from the game for arguing a call.

We drove to Biarritz that afternoon. On the road south I passed a blonde in a yellow Shelby Cobra. She passed me doing about 120. I passed her. She passed me. Lucille slipped down in her seat. She couldn't bear to watch. At the hotel we had a drink in the bar with the blonde. Her name was Doreen and she was vice president of Prudential-Bache. She and Lucille seemed to fancy each other. We agreed to meet later that evening.

Doreen was not at the casino. Lucille and I played a few shoes of bacarrat and drank a bottle of D.P. A few thousand ahead I tipped the croupier well and we left the casino. Lucille drove. She was a little bit drunk. When we arrived at the border the Spanish police made me take the wheel. Lucille was singing a yoghurt jingle in French when we pulled into Arturo's.

When I stopped the car and began to get out Lucille stayed in her seat.

"You are really a shallow guy, do you know that Steve," she said with limpid eyes.

I was hurt but casual. She followed several steps behind me on the flagstone steps to the front door. As I neared the door I turned to tell her to watch her stop in the dark and I paused. Just in front of me a huge wheel of cheese smashed to bits on the naked stone. I looked down at the yellow hunks and realized they could be my brains scattered there.

Someone was trying to kill me.

I told Lucille and she laughed in my face.

"Don't be stupid," she sneered. Then she said something under her breath in Chinese.

"Someone dropped a whole wheel of Gruyere on my head from the top of the chateau," I said.

"Nonsense," said Lucille. "We are near the airport. It fell from a Swissair plane."

The butler came to the door. Ikipope was black and supposedly from New Guinea; to me he looked like Jack Lord, but more effeminate. He had on a dark suit and sandals with socks.

"They've gone, sir," he said blankly.

"Gone where?" I said.

"They didn't say, sir."

Lucille insisted that I drive to a small airfield near the chateau. No one was about. She said we should wait.

"Wait for who?"

She said she didn't know.

I asked her what was in the wallet.

"Identification," she said.

At dawn a single engine plane landed. It taxied to where we were parked.

"Let's go," said Lucille, putting on sunglasses.

"Where?"

"Flying," she said.

As we passed over on take off I glanced at the Gran Turismo and wondered if I would ever see it again. Lucille and I sniffed heroin and my mind wandered into a strange vision where the sound of the engine became the muezzin at a mosque, calling the faithful to prayer. When I came to my senses we were landing on a small desert strip.

The sunlight was blinding as I emerged from the plane, but as soon as I could focus I noticed men sitting on camels. They were carrying rifles. Two of them dismounted and began loading large wheels of cheese into the airplanes—wheels that resembled the one that had nearly killed me.

Without a word being spoken the men lifted Lucille and me on to the backs of camels and as the plane departed we rode off into the dunes, a high mountain range looming in the distance. After half a days ride, during which no one spoke, we arrived at an oasis where there was a large modern house surrounded by a mud brick fence posted with armed guards in Arab dress.

The leader of our caravan took us into the house. When he pulled his burnoose aside I saw that he was a blonde, blue-eyed European, deeply tanned. His name was Dirk. He welcomed me to his house smiling secretively to Lucille. He gave me a cold beer and ordered the major domo to show me to my room.

A turbaned blackamoor motioned me to follow. We walked down a long glass corridor with piped-in music—a large string orchestra playing "Light My Fire."

We came to a heavily curtained door. The huge man gestured for me to enter and I did.

Inside I found Helena and Doreen laying naked on a huge bed feeding one another apricots. They smiled at me.

"How long have you b-been here?" I stammered.

"Since Friday," said Helena.

"It's Sunday," cooed Doreen, "but that doesn't matter."

"The hell it doesn't. I have a meeting with the IRS on Tuesday morning at 8 a.m."

I was at the Cairo airport by nightfall. I found the Avis representative and handed over the keys to the Grand Turismo.

INCUNABULA #3

BY SUSAN DAITCH

People used to read everything as if it were a story. Readers looked for moral tales. They wanted to be taught a lesson and then to move on to the next potential mistake. They matched accidents and natural disasters to hearsay, fables, and myths. It was a way of imposing logic on mishaps. It initiated a system of cross-referential meaning where none would seem to have existed previously. It was a way not to seem like a city of helpless victims hit by random catastrophe. Here was authority. Here was a motive for revenge. People used to read for pleasure. People wanted to recognize the end of a story in its beginning. People wanted to be surprised at its end, anyway.

She grew increasingly afraid to leave her apartment and gave others complicated grocery lists. When they were uncooperative, she would live on coffee with powdered milk and spaghetti sauce eaten directly from the jar with a spoon. Her personal geography grew truncated in proportion to potential fatalities that she associated with runaway subway cars and the crimes she linked to the density of foreigners in the streets. She defined a foreigner as anyone she failed to recognize. The hazards crept towards the door. She would listen to the radio for hours as a substitute for actually doing anything. She approached the act of listening the way another person might consider driving a car or writing a letter. Radio time began to replace clock time. Before noon the news came on five minutes before the hour. That divided the morning into equal parts but added five minutes to the first hour of the afternoon. Friends hoped she might have some reconciliation with at least the front steps of her building before the end of the summer.

I see them working in subways. Blue, green, gold, orange tiles: the front of a locomotive, little houses unlike any seen in metropolitan New York, beavers and squirrels in profile. Each piece has been previously cut to the right shape. There is a signal and they jump onto the platform. They mainly work at night. In the morning a gold stripe, a red bracket, sort of baroque, or a tree has been added. Everything is finally covered by something, there is no space left undecorated. When their work is completed, the tilers move on to another station. The irregularity of their presence during daylight and the danger of their work make them seem like peripatetic tap dancers who put together a different act each night. Even after the signal they behave as if they have all the time in the world. One of them noticed I was missing trains in order to watch them so I got on the next one. Later in the night, after they've gone home, painters come and cover parts of the tiles with tags and pictures. There are ghost stations, entirely painted over, which the train passes between working stops. Sometimes the cars halt in front of one; dimly lit and long out of service. It might move slowly past a series of stations full of pictures: an early form of cinema. In the future all stations will be painted over and all the trains will be slow express trains: the history of cinema advances. A movie with images of trailing comets, rockets, larger-than-life silver letters takes shape. Historically earlier parts will feature words made of bubble letters, in later ones the letters turn angular. This has been called Gothic Futurism. In the depths of each station colored names will give way to jungle landscapes, images of mechanized monsters, caricatures of comic figures. Sequences mimic existing perspective to such an extent that people will be sure they must have missed a corner as the train passes. They will want to repeat the trip, in effect, see the movie again. Even though there is so much to see, tiers of scenery, the train must keep up a certain speed or the effect of animation will be lost.

It had once been exciting to be identified, named, and photographed. This happened to her mother in 1939 when she was eleven and the family was broke. Her mother got a job as Mrs. Modern at the World's Fair in Queens. She worked opposite Mrs. Drudge in the Westinghouse Pavillion. Every morning she put on her costume and went to work. Her picture was in papers and newsreels whenever the Westinghouse Pavillion was discussed. Sometimes she was by herself, sometimes she was photographed with Mrs. Drudge who had no machines and did everything by hand. The whirlagig of sensationalism occasionally included the actual sons and daughters of Mrs. Modern and Mrs. Drudge as they went through their daily lives as real children. A *Life* photographer appeared at her school looking for her. She ducked into the bathroom, spent a few hours there, then ran away. She didn't want to be recognized as a child of Mrs. Modern.

Because she had so little information, written language was all she would trust. Words spread out like puddles of inference, thin at the edges, creeping towards misuse, misspelling, mispronunciation. The boundaries of words grew vague. One impersonated the next. She set up a schemata based on analagous relationships.

All hotels have a few rules in common.

Everyone needs the right clothes.

You must have money in order to live.

Repulsive behavior can take many forms.

She read newspaper lines straight across: "the women wear full length mink major source of permanent housing for the homeless can't ski anywhere in the world without a gold Rolex. Official said the city hoped would not set foot without major gemstones, $49 a day for a family of four"

"It ruined a three-week trip. forced to leave buildings that have been abandoned.
Still other had to leave over-
crowded apartments of"

" 'comes a guy with the latest Italian skiwear. I was proud. I told him,
ments more quickly. Homeless families are now housed in hotels"

"You don't stay in a hotel, you stay in a
what-do-you-call-it? A house."

Iterative clauses hinted at branches of connotation and so she
made diagrams. Antiphrasis struck deaf ears. She had no sense of
irony. She read literally and lines of print gave her a hard time.
She became easily distracted, turned to anther page, confronted
a similar set of lines, felt hungry, struck a match, lit a burner and
boiled water. It was all as discontinuous as the definition of
hotel.

You had to know someone or be with someone who knew
someone in order to get in. A narrow storefront, almost not that,
almost a corridor connecting other corridors that you really
couldn't get into. Sometimes there were a couple of tables and
chairs inside. Sometimes a man (it was not always a man) or two
would be sitting in one of them. If you just walked in off the
street the fat guy behind the counter would tell you in Spanish
that they weren't open for business.
A man I knew was like Mr. Memory in *The 39 Steps*. He would
take risks if you could manage to convince him no one would
guess what he was really doing. No one would believe his inten-
tions were anything but benign, his interests anything but self-
interests. He didn't appear the sort of person easily waylaid by
aimless curiosity. I persuaded him to go in with me because I
couldn't go in by myself. I would be nervous, my teeth would
chatter, I would look at the floor. Like Mr. Memory, he would
know the answers to their questions and if they, like the German

spies in the movie, asked for the formula for a particular airplane engine, he would have recited arbitrary numbers and I'm sure they would have been the correct ones. Neither one of us did get in. I never found out what went on in there.

Like Madeleine Carroll, I didn't want to be attached to the stranger who kissed her/me on the train. As danger became more apparent, she became more cooperative, but in my case, the danger was of my own invention. If we were Madeleine Carroll and Robert Donat handcuffed together, rolling down an embankment, playing elopers at a hotel, then he couldn't be Mr. Memory at the same time. Hero and traitor mixed in the same actor. Possibly the story was skewed. I felt stuck into the wrong character.

He didn't recognize her. He was sitting at a table with other people, looked up at her and then spoke to his friends as if she were no one in particular. She walked close to the group as if she were going to the telephone booth to their right. He didn't look up. She pretended to make a call, put a quarter in the slot and dialed her own number, left a message for herself on the machine. The message made little sense and continued long past the beep. The cord was very long for a phone booth. She turned, winding it around herself so she was facing him but he still didn't recognize her or even notice her. He was wearing a tie with silver horseshoes and horses' heads painted on it. From where she stood the horse heads looked like shiny flies. An unknown woman wrapped in a telephone cord, like Jane Avril wrapped in a snake. She thought she should have made up a conversation instead of leaving a long message on what was actually her own machine but it was too late to change her story. As if anyone who might hear her would stop their own conversation and ask her just what kind of a nut she thought she was. He tapped the table to make a point then, looked out the window as if disgusted or defeated. She couldn't go on just standing there.

The personal things put on each desk grew to monstrous representations of buffoonery. The ashtray with *My Favorite Martian*'s picture embedded in it says goofiness is the large category under which you operate. Even actions committed for sincere reasons, under serious pretense will prove just as embarrassing. The ashtray denies all of this. Your motives can never rise any higher. Other employees have feminized objects on their desks: artificial flowers, birthday cards, picture frames, souvenir lighters. You can't say if these objects are feminized or emasculated because, conceptually, they are relatively neuter. They could have gone either way. A lighter or the idea of a lighter wasn't originally burdened by connotations of gender, at least not in English. A man in the office suggests these objects are emasculated by virtue of combination. He has a paperweight of the Empire State Building embedded in plastic on his desk. When you shake the thing, of course, it snows. The paperweight might be a cliché but he insists it's not femmey. No one suggests to him the that World Trade Center is bigger. I go to another floor to get a cup of coffee out of a fairly neutral-looking machine. I find myself being drawn to the image of cuteness in inert things, but if you relinquish everything to cuteness, you might become happy enough at your job so that you would think twice before leaving it.

She wrote *rue*. No further description was needed. *Rue* was not the same as *rua, via,* or street. She wrote Clinton in front of street, *rue* needed no modifier. It already spoke of balconies, thin curtains, a set of shutters which opened out and a pair of windows which opened in.

Eventually only printed language which had been reproduced had any credibility. She felt like a caretaker of inauthentic documents and she was in search of a nucleus of the original sentence. They were fly-by-night resurrections, none of them to be entirely trusted. Tokens: the resurrections were only traces of some past myth of precision. She had no faith in pictures or photographs. All evidence had to be verbal. She kept stacks of newspapers in mostly chronological order. It was a slow system. She couldn't always find what she was looking for. Her hands and cuffs were often dirty, her forehead smeared with inky tracks.

One subject which never, to her knowledge, appeared in print was her own life. Even its most mundane aspects were never verified by reproduction in newspapers. The stacks under tables and chairs, under her bed, suggested an important simulacrum and one which excluded her.

He told me a story about finding a human hand in a garbage can. I didn't believe him. I know people who find decent furniture and remarkable clothing on the street, but a human hand, never. He was putting off going back to his apartment and would just say anything. He did this every night after work. I asked him what kind of hand it was, what did it look like? Black or white, big or little? Was it holding anything? Was it wearing jewelry? I didn't exactly make a study of it, he said. How do you know if it was real at all? Maybe it was rubber. No, it was real, this was no rubber hand, he was certain. Did you go to the police? No, there was no point, it was just a hand, not a body. Could it have been a prop? You said it wasn't rubber but it might have been something else, some special kind of plastic, for example. Were you walking near a theatre or a prop shop? He was getting annoyed but he didn't want to go home. There are cities where things like this happen and it is considered normal. You don't have to live in Santiago or Buenos Aires to find body parts on the street. But this, I reminded him, is not one of those cities.
Had the hand taken over his life? Had its appearance ruined for him further use? Well, yes, for a few days he had been upset and thought of little else. He couldn't put a plastic bag full of coffee grounds and balled-up pieces of paper, a bag which said, "Have a Nice Day!" on top of a human hand.
He didn't want to go inside his building yet. It was warm and after we separated I knew he'd walk around for hours. If we hadn't worked together that night he would have attached himself to someone else or roamed the street talking to himself.

People have always found before-and-after stories very compelling. The lives of formerly bald, now hairy; or formerly fat, now thin people are automatically read as stories because they prove that anyone can start a new life, regardless of their past. People used to read as a substitute for religion. People used to read if they were patricians. People used to read everything as if were a metaphor, or if not that, as if all the lines contained nothing but tropes. People used to put off the end of the story for as long as possible, putting obstacles between it and the moment at hand, even if they knew how the story would end, and had known its end since they could remember.

LEAVING QUITO

BY GARY INDIANA

"It was difficult to imagine that we were about to see the traces of a glacier thousands of years old. There was a hole in the rock at about the level of the cock of an average-sized man. That we were going to walk in its path and follow its footsteps down into the valley. My fingers trembling, I unzipped my cutoffs, eager to get the confining cloth out of the way. Our feelings before starting our trip to the mountain lakes were dwarfed alongside the magic of a panorama where reality surpasses imagination. As I pushed them down, my hard prick snapped up against my belly and then stood straight out in front of me. Our departure point was Lake Toreadora, 37 kilometers from the city, 3,500 meters above sea level. Fred had unzipped his pants and taken out his cock to arouse Dick more."

Singapur, 28.—"Miss Noruega," Marian Leines; "Miss Hong Kong," Fui Chung y "Miss Suecia," Susanne Thoerngren, constan entre las primeras concursantes que han llegado aquí para el concurso de "Miss Universo," que se realizará el 27 de mayo.

Clouds avalanching down the skin of the volcano. Hard green hills, fissures of gray between the peaks and the bleach white sculptures spread across the sky.

The Inca is *muerte.* The Inca has been enthronized above fat pylons of cedar and palm. The priest of Our Lord, Jésus Christ, baptized the Inca an hour before the auto-da-fe so he did not die heathen by agonizing torture over several days but simply roasted for an hour or two.

At the airport, the far-off crackle of breathy voice, *vuelo,* she sighs, *quanto, Avianca por Lima, Santiago, Valparaiso,* outside the blue air sits gently on the brazen palms.

–That was for us, says the woman idly.

–Yes.

–Senor Carlos. He can help you very much.

Pizarro digs a brown line with the point of his sword: those who wish may advance for the glory of Spain and the Spanish Crown and those base cowards who merely because of affliction with scurvy wish to return to Panama will perhaps live to regret their stupid loss of incalculable riches.

The parrots mock them. The turtles strapped on the sides of their pathetic boats for food mock them even in death, as their heads are severed.

Gloria, Gloria, in excelsis deo: the simple Indian with an orange kerosine tank strapped to her back embraces the feet of the gigantic Christ.

–He's not around?

–I forget what he looks like, really.

The official from the airline approaches, bland and buttery, like a fading cabbage.

–Is that for us?

Yes. You pay the airport tax, and then you will go and get in touch with the young lady from Equitoriana. She knows about you already.

–We just paid for the lunch.

–No. You did not have to.

Blessed art thou among women and blessed is the fruit of thy womb, Jesus.

–Well, they charged us.

Holy Mary, Mother of God, pray for us sinners, now, and at the hour of our death.

–I did it already. I paid.

217

Well, they did.

–They charged you? For the lunch? Come over with me.

Our Father who are in Heaven, hallowed be thy Name.

The flames rise from the stake. Whips of yellow are visible in the emerald hills.

–No, don't worry about it. The plane will be late. But they were not supposed to charge you for the lunch.

Walkie-talkie static, in bursts.

The beloved bastard of the Inca who reigns supreme in Quito, sends an entreaty to Huascar, Supreme Emperor of Cuzco. Atahuallpa wishes to gather, from each of the nations recently conquered by the Inca, mourners for his deceased father. Actually, he plans to marshal troops against Huascar. Huascar, gullible and a fool who thinks he's secure in his Incahood, sends permission via the thousand-mile highway his ancestors have carved through the length and breadth of the incredible Inca Empire.

–Go get your money.

It was 1500 sucres. So, if you want to go—

–I don't, really. It's your money.

–Let's go.

–No, no, it's really okay. We don't mind.

–But I paid for the lunch already.

Pizarro listens to his foul and unworthy interpreter, the lowborn Felipillo, whose liaison with a royal concubine should have caused not only his own death but that of his entire family, his entire tribe. He, Pizarro, examines a tiny, jeweled casket.

–Instead of that, why don't you just get us through without standing in line. And that would be, you know, acceptable.

–Everyone here is waiting. Just a couple of minutes.

–I don't really care about the lunch.

–It's not fair, you know. I already signed for it. Let's go upstairs, it takes two minutes, that's all.

A presentiment of his own assassination tickles Pizarro's forebrain. He knows he will die by the knife, murdered by his own beloved lieutenants. Though he does not love them all that much, even now, for they are a smelly pack of greedy swine. But first he will conquer the Inca, demanding ransom for Atahuallpa in the form of a room stacked to the ceiling with gold.

–I paid. But they charged 1500 sucres.

–For extras, maybe.

–Extras, yes.

–I don't mind.

–Extras.

I want to sleep, Pizzarro thinks: I want to lie down here in the filthy black mud of this island and sleep for one thousand years, without dreaming. The stink of blood I have shed nauseates me. My murders will smell throughout history, like ammonia. I have destroyed an ancient and noble race for no higher motive than the others. I sicken myself: why should I live? Why do they call me a conqueror, when I cannot conquer myself, my own sickening lusts? And then at the end I shall be killed as easily as I now kill that ridiculous bird up there in the lofty tree.

–The plane just arrived. You have to be patient. We have to fix the plane, we have to do many things. You still have time.

–Okay.

–It doesn't take that long. Twenty minutes, we will be there.

–There's a departure tax?

–Yes. It was only $5 two months ago. But now, twenty.

–What's the equivalent in sucres?

–Each dollar has 170 sucres. You forgot something?

A bird with a pink and yellow bill, high above, cocking its dumb shrunken bead and watching my death.

–It's usually three bucks.

–Twenty is a lot.

–Okay, maybe I have it in sucres.

–You probably do.

–Dollars?

–Check your tickets, though. Because it says departure card on them. Or it should.

As I lie dying I would of course remember, not the triumphs of all my many glories, but the evening Ruiz and I drank a gallon of palm wine, vomiting throughout the jungle, and after some hours Ruiz leers and asks me: I'm curious, did you ever fuck a dog?

–I can't wait for the age of teleportation . . . and I'll never go on Equitoriana if they ever get teleport machines.

–They'd probably get a fly in there with you.

–Your legs will be here some time this week.

–That will be a mess, probably. Losing parts of people, sending them to the wrong place.

–Wrong place, and putting them on the wrong bodies.

–And if you lose your ticket, you're really in trouble.

–Then you'll be nowhere. Your genes will be floating around in space.

–So what else is there, besides Quito, Guyaquil, and Cuenca?

–Isn't that enough?

–There's Esmeraldas, where blacks live, which I guess is in the north. There's also little places, of course. In the disputed territories.

–And that Virgin on the hill. Quito. What a trip.

–Virginity is a big item around here, also.

–Very prized.

–Well, of course, they used to sacrifice them.

–That's why they built the statue so big. That's the last Virgin, she's too big for the Volcano.

–The Aluminum Virgin. It was really quite interesting, getting inside her. They have stained glass windows, and then all these figures of different Indian types holding spears, and stuffed iguanas.

–They said the Incas had destroyed Quito. They razed it to the ground. And then it was rebuilt in the 1500s.

–I don't believe the original inhabitants of any place would be the destroyers of it.

–Yes, but the Incas actually conquered the people who were here before. And the people who were here were fighting the Incas. I mean, that's what it says in that guidebook, but there are many things wrong in that guidebook.

–So did you have to leave the VIP area to go to the bathroom?

–I spoke already to the stewardess. She is going to give you good attention, some wine and stuff, and special attention, okay?

–We board the aircraft?

–TAME?

–Not TAME. Tam-ay.

–That's the one that crashed.

–The cannibals got the passengers. The survivors. TAME. Tam-ay. Where did it crash, that the cannibals got them?

–In the woods, in Colombia.

–And here.

–Look. Nuns.

–Wasn't it a shampoo? TAME? No, it was a creme rinse, now that I think of it. It's a shame to shampoo without TAME.

–I never went to a duty-free shop before.

Thy kingdom come, thy will be done, on earth as it is in heaven. I can never repent so many homicides.

–Did you buy anything?

–Yes, I got some, what do you call those things?

–Scarves. And Jose Llopez cigars, apparently. I got three scarves, and that bag there. I thought I'd gotten something else, too. Well, I guess it's just the three scarves.

Okay. Because this plane is coming from Mexico, your seat will be unassigned until Guyaquil. Then in Guyaquil, you take your own seat, okay? Could we go in first class? They have certain passengers in Panama, getting on. Do we change planes? No, but until Guyaquil you take any seat. Well. If there were going to be one more complication, I'm sure they would come up with it. Did I tell you? I got this jacket here. I kept going to all these shops, always closed. I got this sweater, and this. I was flying high. It was hard for me to believe that a small town like mine could offer so much hot male sex. The villages became more numerous, and, as the vessels rode at anchor off the port of Tacamez, the Spaniards saw before them a town of two thousand houses or more, laid out into streets, and it suddenly seemed to me that every man in town was gay. This was not true, of course. She looked out and saw this guy naked, bound to a post, with a belt being cracked across his bare butt. She called the cops. I got this sweater, and this. When the royal procession had arrived within half a mile of the city, it came to a halt; and Pizarro saw with surprise that Atahuallpa was preparing to pitch his tents. My heart pounded. Bill was nothing to sneeze at. Better than six feet tall, as blond as Hank, but a year or two younger. His body was great, too. I saw his tight ass outlined in the overalls and wondered if Hank had ever screwed him. Now, this is definitely special treatment right here. We have our own Equitoriana umbrella, so in other words, there's going to be mob scene on this airplane. We just keep walking endlessly along these tarmacs from one plane to another, one taxi to another, one restaurant to another. Doing absolutely nothing. I wonder if we can keep the umbrella. It would be quite impressive to those who have never flown Equitoriana. Where do you live? In New York. No, I know, but where, in Chinatown? Park Avenue South, by Union Square. Where do you live? Twelfth Street. Right nearby, actually. Oh I think we can unfurl, or rather furl it. Got it? Do you want to sit by the window? Yes, if you don't. Oh. The L.A. Times. "Fatal Chase." Sounds pretty good. Ladies and gentlemen, welcome to Guyaquil. Information, 15 hours, 39 degrees centigrade. Somebody spilled 4711. What? You know that cologne? 4711? Oh. I don't get it. From Mexico to Quito, then to Guyaquil, and then to Panama? God, I hope a lot of people don't get on this plane. Bill unzipped the front of his coveralls, revealing a broad chest with huge pectoral blocks, crowned by beautifully formed rosy nipples and a scattering of golden fuzz. The scene for this second auto-da-fe at Valladolid was the great square before the church of St. Francis. At one end a platform was raised, covered with rich carpeting, on which were ranged the seats of the inquisitors, emblazoned with arms of the holy office. I licked my lips greedily, thinking of how good the hot cock meat was going to taste. It was going to be great sucking it into my gullet, taking time to taste the flavor of every inch of it. I think we're in the right seats as it is. I think we're in the same seats as on our boarding passes. You'll have to move. No, because we're in the right seats anyhow. Where's your seat. *Cago en tus muertos,* which means I shit on your dead relatives. That's pretty good. I wish that child would shut up. It seems a lot of people are getting off. Why don't we watch there, maybe they're taking off our luggage. Put that back on the plane, would you? I'd be willing to just forget it, at this point. That looks like mine. No. Ours have little pink tags on them. Mine doesn't have little rollers on the bottom. No, but there are pink tags on ours. Looks like something leaked on that one. Looks like something leaked on all of them. No, they all look wet. Missionaries. Just what this country needs. They're bringing the word. Trash. Too late now. Looks like a mummy. That's like the bodies we saw on the road. We going to Panama, now? Panama to New York. From Mexico, figure that one out. Straight from Panama to New York. Unless they go to Peru. So, I wonder what time. That does look like my bag over there. Where? The one on top. You have a strap on top of yours. Yeah. No, but it's not the same type of strap. Maybe I can see when they turn it around. No, it's not mine. And if you see your bag going off, what can you do? You run out. At this point, let it go. Well, that must have been the last of the luggage. Now they're taking the packages off. What's that ring? Garnet. I went to price rubies at Stearn? For a quarter of a carat they wanted two-and-a-half-thousand dollars. Is that okra? Sure they're not peppers? They probably are. No, they're okras. No. Okay, pepper. Those are the box lunches. Excuse me? Is Sylvia back from lunch? I really don't know. We were supposed to be in first class, but there was a problem with the tickets. So we have priority. Sylvia knows about it. It is okra, look. I didn't know we imported okra from Panama. You have your tickets? Our tickets mean nothing, because they're made out for the 25th. We were supposed to receive priority treatment. My prick jerked around, standing up hard and firm as a candle. The sensations ran right up my legs and into my nuts. In the hurry of the flight of one party, and the pursuit by the other, all pouring towards Cuzco, the field of battle had been deserted. But it soon swarmed with plunderers, as the Indians, descending like vultures from the mountains, took possession of the bloody ground, and, despoiling the dead, even to the minutest article of dress, left their corpses naked on the plain. Time and information are abstract concepts, mere memories of days past. But you know what's funny, when we got to Quito, we started going back to New York time. In Cuenca we were living on Cuenca time. You kind of have to, in Cuenca. Actually, to tell you the truth, once you get ready to leave you don't feel like going. I don't know if it's the traveling, or what.

LOU **ROBINSON**

EXTREMES OF HIGH & LOW REGARD

TOP STORIES #27 $3.00

EXTREMES
OF HIGH
AND LOW
REGARD

LOU ROBINSON

NAMING THE URGE

My real name is Jo, after my mother's favorite character in *Little Women*. She was named for Catherine in *Wuthering Heights*. My mother hated Catherine and changed her name to Mona when she was thirteen. My grandmother confessed to having been torn between Catherine and Fanny, another heroine, but back then her husband could still put his foot down. She herself was christened Elsie, which I loved, but my grandmother hated because of Elsie the Borden cow. She started the grandchildren calling her Hazel, after a pagan novel by Mary Webb. Babies heard that as Hey Zel, so it got shortened to Zel.

Early impressed by the arbitrary, malleable nature of naming, I jettisoned Jo for Stormy, the name of a horse in a book I once read that had a cover portrait of a yearling with a wild, blue-black mane. Other names I had considered: Seal, Smoky, Micah, Coaly Bay, Blue, Cinnamon, Sorrel, all the colors horses come in.

Stormy seemed to leave more room for temperament.

My family are all great readers, to the point of rudeness. We'd drive all the way to Vandalia to visit Zel, make straight for the magazine rack and retreat with a stack that would take us through dinner to bedtime. It wasn't hard to change your name. The general atmosphere was one of detached indulgence. Whenever they looked up from their books, it was with faces of surprise and amusement, as if they truly were confused about my origins. I propped my comic books on a solid shelf of bitter chocolate, like a lap desk, nibbling and sucking the edge all day. Zel had taken a machete and carved off this slab for me from the dark bitter wall of chocolate that stood ten feet high in the cold room.

The magazine rack was in the store attached to the house that Zel and her husband, Moss, owned—a grocery store and soda fountain called Lane's Confectionary. It was the very womb of luxury. I fed myself from the soda fountain: chocolate coke for breakfast, cherry coke with lunch (a hot dog in crinkly cellophane heated in the machine), banana coke with dinner. I whipped around behind the counter, pulling parrot head fountain spouts, spooning balls of ice cream into giant soda glasses, topping off root beer froth, to the deep envy of neighborhood kids. Kids loved my grandfather Moss. They called him Laney. He was a small wiry man in a long white apron and white fitted cap over thick vanilla hair, who worked from dawn to dusk. His silence, and the whiteness of his hair were due to the war, after which he had become a ghost, handing out free candy and running up bills for the whole neighborhood all through the depression straight into bankruptcy. In a photograph he stands in front of the big wavy mirror behind the fountain, in eternal apron and cap, his skinny arms holding an eighty-pound candy cane under his chin like a barbell. Above, his eyes are absent, or spooked. Each Christmas Laney gave one of these monster candy canes away to whoever could guess its weight.

It was strenuous work, candymaking. In his basement workroom he would punch and roll the mass of hot sugar, heave it over a

227

buttered hook fastened six feet up on a post and pull it, heave and pull. Then separate a great wad of it, make a dent with his fist, and Zel would pour in dye so red it was color seen only on the big screen, staining the lips of Anne Bolyn. Then he would roll and twist this ruby wad into a stripe of perfect evenness against the shiny ivory of the rest.

Meanwhile Zel did all the smaller candies that lined the glass case upstairs in the store. Fondant, nougat, turtles, chocolate caramels and creams. I helped, pressing walnuts into caramels to make legs and head, dipping them in their baths of milky tan or bitter cocoa. Sometimes Zel made candy bars named after her grandchildren: the Lynn-bar, the Candy-bar, the Jo-bar. People came from all over the Midwest for their candy. That meant each holiday Zel and Moss nearly killed themselves getting the orders ready, running the store at the same time. All the relatives came to help.

These are my secret memories of bliss. The long line of them in white aprons and caps, perched on tall green stools, their elbows moving in and out in unison as they roll the slender fairy sticks forward and back, forward and back to round and cool them. Every pastel color and every sweet hot smell you could imagine and nothing forbidden. When I felt the need to dream in a little more privacy, I could work alone in the cold room, coloring in the mules on the Lane's Cough Drop boxes—red for cherry, brown for horehound.

Easter was the holiday the adults dreaded most, but it was the height of Zel's magical power. Her simple painted boiled eggs were beyond description. Silver-green paisleys like the cloth she remembered from Scotland. Deep purple pansies edged with chrome yellow. Cornflower blue bachelor buttons, each tiny frond distinct, each hair on the moss-green stem bristling.

Easter morning I would rise to find the basket—three feet high, wrapped in cellophane and tied with a mauve satin ribbon, the basket itself sometimes made of woven candy, shiny, eggshell white. Inside, deep green grass pillowed one giant chocolate egg covering the smoothest butter cream. No other candy-maker came close to the texture of Zel's creams. Its chocolate surface was covered with blue and lavender flower petals, ivy, and *Stormy* written in a sweeping script of the palest yellow frosting. Around it—rainbow fairy sticks, little marshmallow chicks in a smaller basket of woven pink fondant, pale green sea-foam pieces, deep crimson cinnamon suckers as clear as stained glass. And the hollow egg. A fairy-tale object, made from a blown goose egg coated with layers of sugar tinted all the pale colors of snow under church lights. Through the window the size of a thumbnail, a tiny Stormy could be seen standing beside blue-green pine trees, holding the reigns of a miniature licorice horse. In the grass at her feet, rabbits, cats, wildflowers and Easter eggs the size of Indian belt beads.

It wasn't just that my grandmother had renamed herself—effecting a window, a slim hope. Or that her art was both inspired and generous, created only to be devoured. She demonstrated that you could change yourself to fit your private dream. Her vanity table covered in wild blue and pink flowered chintz, holding buns of hair from her childhood that she sometimes attached to her loose strawberry waves with long blond hairpins. Bedside table covered with astrology magazines, movie star magazines, Christian Science pamphlets, and novels by women. Opinionated, haughty, she existed to recreate the sordid everyday, passing this talent along to her daughter and granddaughter. My mother took as her motto Scarlet's line "I'll think about it tomorrow." A positive construction was built over every blow, every warp or sharp odor.

Standing in front of the mirror at the foot of the stairs, age four. A chance wind has blown a piece of hair over, giving me the idea to part it in the middle for once. The pleasure of staring at yourself, changing yourself. Suddenly a tomboy with a serious look becomes a doe, a cameo with a widow's peak. Who would not want to hold her to them forever? Simple as that, I think, sly behind my new look of acquiescence. A whole new character grows from a single image. Now there are two: one with which to combat; one with which to seduce. The new one gets a secret name: Cat.

Naming flows from the source of lost possibilities. You name someone, you put your hopes for them into the word, shaping a little cage. When you name yourself you form a cage perhaps of smaller dimensions than your mother would have imagined for you.

My naming urge became fierce, creating apocryphal tokens that I would roam behind for years.

MARY KELLY

PECUNIA NON OLET

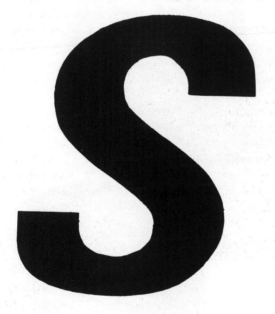

South on 15, east on 8, exit offramp 94. Potrero, Campo, Jacumba, then nothing. The foothills ground down to a solemn flatness. She looked at the map. Turn left, six miles to the reservoir, windmill on the right, slowdown. There it was. Huge gawking hacienda surrounded by a metal fence, snarling barbed wire at the rim. It looked abused, once elegant veranda, ornate tiles now weathered, cracked. Imagining the Spanish with their clavichords and lacquered armoires, she portaged her stereo and her answering machine to the entrance with propriety. It belonged to her. Four thousand feet of open space for next to nothing. Unthinkable back in the city where she should be, but at last she could see several paintings at the same time and afford to have assistants. They would be grateful to work here. Although, she had been told to keep a gun, not to shoot, of course, to show them she meant business. Business, yes, she would do business. She would be discovered, wild woman painter of, well, forty-eight, no child prodigy, but ambitious nevertheless. She would entertain in her capacious monument—vaulted ceiling and expansive walls, high windows, ample frames, each painted white. The table laid, her ivory candels would disburse their shrewd titanium light, and guests, all wearing black, would chant "great space, great space."

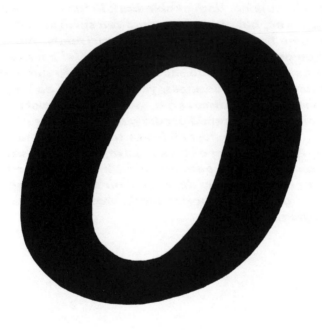

WHAT'S THE FASTEST WAY TO MAKE A MILLION?

Crime, yeah, that's the only way. Should be stylish though, let's see . . . you could make a perfect replica of a night-time deposit box, graft it carefully onto the bank's facade and then remove it several hours later with substantial contents. Beautiful, what d'ya think?

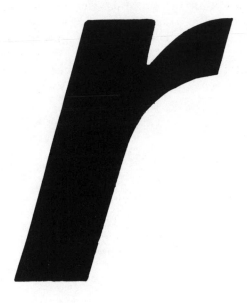

Someday, when she was older, she would leave the city. Leave the dirt, fumes, noise, etcetera, and move to the country. There, she would live simply, grow her own alfalfa, zucchini, tomatoes, and so forth, and savor the last morsels of unpolluted air before they escaped through the terrible hole. Meanwhile, she resolved to invest her savings in a plot of land, upstate—small lake, tall pines, rolling hills, and so on. She could not afford to build a house, but at least she could go there on week-ends with a tent, a picnic basket, and a friend—ideally, an architect—and plan. Where to begin—perhaps a swimming pool and two cabanas, the rest would come later, later when she was ready to leave the city, when she was older, and if she met the right person. Until then, she decided to put on her leather jacket, chain bracelets, lace ankelts and the like, and live complexly a little longer.

ATHLETIC Attractive 48 yr old prof. woman, terrific sense of humor. Looking for honest, healthy, successful, WF, sincere relationship, age 40-60, no smoking, no losers, no tattoos.

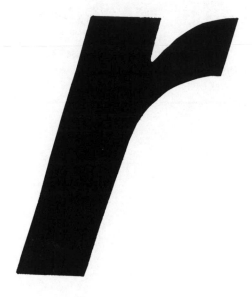

She wanted her <u>and</u> she wanted all of her clothes.

TOP STORIES
1979-1990

1. TOO GOOD TO BE ENTIRELY TRUE by Donna Wyszomierski 1979
2. WORDS IN REVERSE by Laurie Anderson 1979
3. 3 STORIES by Pati Hill 1979
4. AGENT PINK by Suzanne Johnson 1980
5. FOOT FACTS by Linda Neaman 1980
6. THIS IS MY MOTHER. THIS IS MY FATHER. by Gail Vachon 1980
7. EATING FRIENDS by Jenny Holzer/Peter Nadin 1981
8. TRANSCRIPT by Judith Doyle 1981
9. N.Y.C. IN 1979 by Kathy Acker 1981
10. LIVING WITH CONTRADICTIONS by Lynne Tillman/ Drawings by Jane Dickson 1982
11. MARIE by Kirsten Thorup 1982
12. SHATTERED ROMANCE by Janet Stein 1982
13. REAL FAMILY STORIES by Anne Turyn 1982
14. 95 ESSENTIAL FACTS by Lee Eiferman 1982
15. I.T.I.L.O.E. by Constance DeJong 1983
16. ANALECTS OF SELF-CONTEMPT/SWEET CHEAT OF FREEDOM by Ursule Molinaro 1983
17. THE HUMAN HEART by Romaine Perin 1983
18. FORGET ABOUT YOUR FATHER & OTHER STORIES by Donna Wyszomierski 1983
19-20. HOW TO GET RID OF PIMPLES by Cookie Mueller 1984
21. RED MOON/RED LAKE by Ascher/Straus 1984
22. THE COLORIST by Susan Daitch 1985
23-24. FIVE by Constance DeJong, Joe Gibbons, Tama Janowitz, Richard Prince, and Leslie Thornton 1986
25-26. TOURIST ATTRACTIONS by Douglas Blau, Linda L. Cathcart, Cheryl Clarke, Susan Daitch, Constance DeJong, Robert Fiengo, Gary Indiana, Suzanne Jackson, Caryl Jones-Sylvester, Judy Linn, Micki McGee, Glenn O'Brien, Sekou Sundiata, Lynne Tillman, and Jane Warrick 1987
27. EXTREMES OF HIGH AND LOW REGARD by Lou Robinson 1988
28. WAR COMICS by Lisa Bloomfield 1989
29. PECUNIA NON OLET by Mary Kelly 1990

CITY LIGHTS PUBLICATIONS

Herron, Don. THE LITERARY WORLD OF SAN FRANCISCO
Higman, Perry, transl. LOVE POEMS FROM SPAIN AND
    SPANISH AMERICA
Jaffe, Harold. EROS: ANTI-EROS
Kerouac, Jack. BOOK OF DREAMS
Kerouac, Jack. SCATTERED POEMS
Lacarrière, Jacques. THE GNOSTICS
La Duke, Betty. COMPANERAS: Women, Art & Social
    Change in Latin America
La Loca, ADVENTURES ON THE ISLE OF ADOLESCENCE
Lamantia, Philip. MEADOWLARK WEST
Lamantia, Philip. BECOMING VISIBLE
Laughlin, James. THE MASTER OF THOSE WHO KNOW
Laughlin, James. SELECTED POEMS: 1935-1985
Le Brun, Annie. SADE: A SUDDEN ABYSS
Lowry, Malcolm. SELECTED POEMS
Marcelin, Philippe-Thoby. THE BEAST OF THE HAITIAN HILLS
Masereel, Frans. PASSIONATE JOURNEY
Mayakovsky, Vladimir. LISTEN! EARLY POEMS
Mrabet, Mohammed. THE BOY WHO SET THE FIRE
Mrabet, Mohammed. THE LEMON
Mrabet, Mohammed. LOVE WITH A FEW HAIRS
Mrabet, Mohammed. M'HASHISH
Murguía, A. & B. Paschke, eds. VOLCAN: Poems from Central America
O'Hara, Frank. LUNCH POEMS
Paschke, B. & D. Volpendesta, eds. CLAMOR OF INNOCENCE
Pasolini, Pier Paolo. ROMAN POEMS
Pessoa, Fernando. ALWAYS ASTONISHED
Poe, Edgar Allan. THE UNKNOWN POE
Porta, Antonio. KISSES FROM ANOTHER DREAM
Prévert, Jacques. PAROLES
Purdy, James. THE CANDLE OF YOUR EYES
Purdy, James. IN A SHALLOW GRAVE
Purdy, James. GARMENTS THE LIVING WEAR
Rey-Rosa, Rodrigo. THE BEGGAR'S KNIFE
Rigaud, Milo. SECRETS OF VOODOO
Saadawi El, Nawal. MEMOIRS OF A WOMAN DOCTOR
Sawyer-Lauçanno, Christopher, transl. THE DESTRUCTION
    OF THE JAGUAR
Sclauzero, Mariarosa. MARLENE
Serge, Victor. RESISTANCE
Shepard, Sam. MOTEL CHRONICLES
Shepard, Sam. FOOL FOR LOVE & THE SAD LAMENT OF PECOS BILL
Smith, Michael. IT A COME
Snyder, Gary. THE OLD WAYS
Solnit, Rebecca. SECRET EXHIBITION: Six California Artists
    of the Cold War Era
Solomon, Carl. MISHAPS PERHAPS
Solomon, Carl. MORE MISHAPS
Turyn, Anne, ed. TOP TOP STORIES
Tutuola, Amos. FEATHER WOMAN OF THE JUNGLE
Tutuola, Amos. SIMBI & THE SATYR OF THE DARK JUNGLE
Valaoritis, Nanos. MY AFTERLIFE GUARANTEED
Wilson, Colin. POETRY AND MYSTICISM